LOHSIE'S WOODS

Story by Eric Carl Artherhults

Cover art by Heather Maranda
With illustrations by Daniel Bookmiller
Special thanks to Ed Trail

AMY –
HAPPY READING!

1

Muse,

I feel a longing in my soul that keeps you safe in my heart always. A longing that years, nor miles, could ever diminish. If I were to climb the highest mountain and shout to the sky, it would be your name that would echo through the valleys for all eternity.

In loving memory of

Dougie, Michael and Denny Ferguson

Table of Contents

JUST FOR FUN! Try to answer the questions at the end of the book to see how well you know Art and his friends. If you answer them all correctly it means you are in "the club"! If you don't answer any of them correctly it means you didn't read the book!

PART ONE - LOHSIE'S WOODS

Arthur Carlson laughed when the deejay introduced the next song as an oldie but a goody. "C'mon, that song isn't *that old*...," he thought as he glanced into the mirror. "Has it been that long?" Thinking back and doing the math, he came up with the sobering answer... thirty years! He laughed in disbelief that a song so dear to him, one that represented his youth, could be thirty years old!

Arthur smiled at the thought as drops of rain began to fall. The familiar landscape of Fort Wayne, Indiana unfolded before him as he got closer to the place of his birth. The good times came to mind, the long days spent with the old gang of kids that grew up in the neighborhood of Lohsie's Woods. The memories poured down on him one thought after another, bombarding him in quick flashes. Childhood events he hadn't thought about in years suddenly revealed themselves as if they happened just yesterday. He realized that many of the things that seemed so important and frightening to him as a child were now laughable.

But there was a time when things were different, when everything that happened in life was new and exciting. A time when the world was only as large as the block that you lived on, kids stayed out until the streetlights came on, and parents warned kids to stay out of Lohsie's Woods...

OLD MAN LOHSIE

Every kid on the block believed that Mr. Lohsie killed kids. He had a laboratory in his house and tortured children that dared to enter his woods. Kids have gone in looking for lost baseballs and never came back out! At least that's the story Mitch Bauer told Phil and Art.
"Why else would he dig big holes in his back yard and then fill them back in? What are you guys, stupid?"
"Nuh-uh, Bauer you lie!" Phil mumbled in disbelief.

"Yeah, you lie." Art agreed.

"Well, if you don't believe me just look for yourselves." The boys followed his gaze. Sure enough, there in the clearing of Lohsie's woods was a freshly dug hole. Beside it was a mound of black dirt. Bauer seemed to be telling the truth, the hole was proof. "See guys! I told you so."

This impossible suggestion was fascinating to Phil and Art. It wasn't just a pile of dirt left over from putting in a new septic tank, as Phil first suggested. Bauer had told them that was a stupid idea. They decided to be *smart* and not question him. Staring blankly at the five foot tall mound, Art whispered to Phil, "I think he's lying'..."

Not just an imaginative storyteller, Bauer was also a born vandal. He enjoyed destroying other people's property. So when he wandered away, it didn't surprise Art to find him throwing rocks at Mr. Lohsie's metal shed. Phil and Art half-heartedly joined in, both keeping a cautious eye out for danger. Lohsie could be anywhere, at any time. He had a special knack for popping up out of thin air. When that happened the kids were frozen with fear and rendered speechless. Except for Bauer, whose first impulse was to say words the other kids weren't allowed to say... bad words.

The greatest thing about bombarding the metal shed with rocks and cinders was the explosive sounds it made. The resounding thuds and reverberations of the metal made their hearts leap. Art, who had been appointed "look out", was busy searching for the perfect throwing rock when the shed door swung open. Lohsie's looming presence filled the void. Time stopped. Everyone froze, staring hopelessly until Bauer broke the trance. "LOHSIEEEE!!!" Bauer's voice rang throughout the neighborhood. Art took off like a shot, heart pounding nearly out of his chest with every step. Phil was right on his heels until they cut through the bushes leading to his house. Phil went straight into his back door as Art made a bee-line for a tree. Bauer was nowhere to be seen. He'd been ditched.

Climbing higher and higher into the tree, Art felt safe and well hidden. Here, up in this secret place, he could see his whole world – the entire block – but no one could see him. With the watchful eye of a hawk he scanned the horizon. Down the cement alley he could see the top of Bauer's apple tree. Hinson's basketball court was across from that. Next to that was Addison's house, separated only by an ominous fence from Lohsie's woods. Art breathed a sigh of relief. Bauer had told them that Lohsie never left his property to capture kids. He would appear at the fence and growl things in a language that only another ogre could understand, then turn and disappear into the woods.

SPOILED AND ROTTEN

Some of the stories that Bauer told seemed too unbelievable to be true. But he was the self-appointed boss of the neighborhood. He was one year older and looked smarter because he wore eyeglasses. To Phil and Art, this gave Bauer credibility worthy of respect. It was the kind of respect that made them ignore their own common sense, simply because "Bauer said so!" There was one more important reason that Art and Phil listened to Bauer… he had the best toys.

Bauer had the first Hot Wheels collection, the first air hockey game and the first Rock 'em, Sock 'em Robots on the block. The other kids thought Bauer was the richest kid in the whole wide world. He wore a watch when he was in the third grade. And not just a normal watch, either. With his watch he could tell you what time it was in other parts of world! Even China! He even had that electric football game where the little plastic players jiggled around on the field when you plugged it in. Bauer had his own bank account and carried his own key to his house for when his parents weren't home to let him in. Bauer the bully had it all.

WHAT A GLORIOUS DAY

Saturday was a day full of adventure for the kids that lived in the neighborhood. The screen door slammed behind Art. Without slowing down he grabbed his baseball mitt off the lawn chair and sprinted away. Dodging rosebushes and jumping a hedgerow, Art plowed through the garden of sunflowers and out onto the cinder alley. Stopping to tie his shoe, he told himself to be brave... Lohsie's woods lay ahead.

The morning sun was shining, birds were chirping and the sweet scent of lilacs filled the air. Even the wild flowers in Lohsie's woods were in bloom. In the distance the ice cream truck's familiar chimes beckoned.

Art walked with confidence down the cinder alley, kicking the chunks of stone into the air with each step. Humming the theme song to Batman he clutched the mitt tightly and started into a jog. The jog turned into a full-fledged run by the time he rounded the turn onto the white cement alley. With arms and legs pumping, he glanced over at Lohsie's woods to see if the old man was anywhere in sight. It wasn't until he cut through Phil's bushes that he slowed down to catch his breath.

Bounding up onto Phil's back porch, Art made his presence known by pounding on the screen door. KNOCK! KNOCK! KNOCK! KNOCK!

Phil burst through the door, nearly knocking Art to the ground. Throwing his mitt down on the picnic table, Phil began his own preparation for playing baseball catch. He tucked in his tee shirt and swung his throwing arm round and round like the pitchers he had seen on television. Art was nervously rearranging the padding in the catcher's glove when he heard the pounding sounds of a construction crew. "It sounds like it's coming from Bauer's house." Looking up he noticed that Phil had heard it too.

"It sounds like-"

"Shhh! Phil snapped, listening intently.

Art mumbled on to himself "sounds like Bauer's dad is buildin' him a tree house."

BAUER'S TREEHOUSE

Bauer was in the yard collecting apples and wearing a tool belt and hard hat when the boys got there. Two men were pounding away at planks on the ground. One man was up in the tree sawing away at a branch.

"Everybody get back! Everybody back! Bauer commanded.

Phil looked around and shouted, "Bauer, we ARE everybody!"

"Then stand back and don't touch any of the apples that fall in MY YARD 'cause they're MINE!"

Phil and Art could see Bauer's empire growing right before their very eyes. The tree house was just another thing that he had that they didn't. With it he was sure to be unbearable. Having seen enough, they left Bauer and headed back to Phil's house to play catch. Phil was a left-handed pitcher, and could throw fastballs all afternoon – or until Art quit because his hand was numb.

SNITCH!

Bauer caught up with Phil and Art later, after he'd tired of watching the crew labor on the tree house. He found them looking over the picket fence that stood by Mr. Hankey's property. Wasting no time, Bauer took an awkward swing with his baseball bat and knocked one of the boards cleanly off its top nail. Pleased with this he stepped forward again.

"Count is full, bases are loaded, and here's the pitch..." Bauer whacked it again. CRACK! "HOME RUN," Bauer shouted as the board tumbled to the ground with a hollow thud.

"You're turn, Art," Bauer challenged, handing him the bat. Art looked around for Mr. Hankey. He owned

Hankey's Lot. He was nice enough to let the neighborhood kids use it as a football field. Something just didn't seem right about smashing in his fence. Art thought for a moment, "Let's forget about the fence. Let's play home run derby, you guys. You want to, Phil?" Phil stood, frozen, and mumbled, "You guys..." An angry voice boomed out, "HEY! What are you kids doing?"

 Phil shouted, "Mr. Hankey!" Art turned to look at Bauer but he was gone, Phil high-tailed it too. By the time Art could swing around he felt a vice-like grip on his arm. Bauer had done it again, made a clean escape. Considering the situation Art pleaded for his life. "BAUER DID IT! BAUER DID IT! He lives on Baxter Street. I'LL SHOW YOU HIS HOUSE!" Realizing that he was left holding the bat, he dropped it at Mr. Hankey's feet. Angrily, Hankey growled, "Bauer, huh? I'll get that little brat." Poor Art grabbed the baseball bat and scampered off as the fuming man leaned over to pick up the broken boards.

 The fleeing boy got to the edge of Lohsie's woods just as Phil climbed out from behind a garbage can. "What happened, Art? Did he get Bauer too?" "No. Of course not! Bauer never gets caught! Art screamed back, shaking and red with anger. Phil giggled. He had never seen his friend so mad.

"Shut up, Phil! It's not funny!"

Still fleeing the scene of the crime, the boys crawled through a break in the fence that stood before them. Phil kept his mouth shut for a while to let Art cool off.

THE WOOD PILE

All the excitement had distracted them because, before they knew it, they found themselves halfway into Lohsie's woods. Lohsie's house looked decrepit and void of life. The boys had once agreed that, at night, the old wooden house had the eerie grin of a Halloween pumpkin. Day or night, it gave them the creeps. The broad daylight helped to give them a sense of security. Phil started talking again. Art swung the baseball bat back and forth like a sickle as he scoured the high grass for stray baseballs.

Phil was telling his favorite baseball story, the one about how Babe Ruth pointed out where he was going to smack a homer – when they came upon a woodpile that rose high over their heads. Like a mountain goat, Phil started climbing. Leaping from log to log, he continued his story. "...then the Babe rounded home plate and went straight over to the

14

press box, grabbed the microphone and announced, 'That homer for a little boy that's in the hospital .'" At that moment Phil's weight shifted. His left leg disappeared between two logs. Following closely behind, Art took one more step, putting more weight on the logs that were now crushing Phil's leg.

Phil shrieked out in pain. Realizing their predicament, Art jumped off the woodpile in a panic, leaving the baseball bat behind. Phil's eyes bulged as he realized his predicament. His leg was stuck, maybe even broken, and they were all alone in Lohsie's woods. There was no time to lose. Art started tearing away at the pile of logs, throwing them recklessly from side to side. Phil continued wailing, his pale complexion turning beet red as the pain intensified. As the last log was rolled to the side freeing Phil's injured leg – they heard a screen door slam. LOHSIE! Neither actually saw the old man, but better safe than sorry. Both boys turned tail and ran screaming without looking back. Art raced ahead while pulling Phil like a streamer behind him, sobbing with every painful step.

Bauer was waiting behind the bushes surrounding Phil's backyard. Art appeared first, then Phil, limping like a weary G.I. Joe. Torn jeans covered his once white Red Ball Jet shoes, now brown from the struggle with the logs.

"What happened, you guys?"
Phil said nothing, just limped by, sobbing loudly even after he disappeared into his house. Bauer and Art stood and listened to the muffled crying and wondered about his injured leg. Bauer turned to Art, "Think it's broken? It looked broken."

  By suppertime Bauer had ridden his bicycle around the whole neighborhood shouting the gossip, "MR. LOHSIE BROKE PHIL'S LEG!"

DEAD MEAT

  The next day, Phil's leg was checked out by a doctor who assured him that it wasn't broken. Back in the neighborhood, Bauer's mom ran into one very angry Mr. Hankey. He pumped her gas at the filling station and mentioned that her son had destroyed part of his fence. She was furious. Bauer was immediately grounded.

During this time he had plenty of time to sit and stew. And the more he stewed, the more he turned his hatred toward Art for snitching on him. Then he remembered something... his baseball bat. That was the last straw. Bauer ran to his window where he could see the gang of kids playing in the street. He was so boiling mad the he tried to jerk the window open but got it stuck half-way.

Through the partially open window he screamed at the top of his lungs... "Art! YOU'RE DEAD MEAT, YOU SNITCH! I WANT MY BASEBALL BAT!" The gang froze, everyone looking toward Art. "Uh-oh, you're going to get it now, Art."

Art felt numb. He realized where that bat was, back in Lohsie's woods at the woodpile. "Dead meat..." Art didn't want to be "dead meat". He had one week before Bauer got ungrounded, and only that time to muster up the courage to sneak back to the woodpile and find Bauer's bat.

TROUBLE AHEAD

One week later Bauer slammed Art into the chain-link fence, nearly knocking his own glasses off in the process. "Where is it, Art? I want my bat back, and I want it now!"

Art squirmed to get free. Everyone was watching but no one stepped in to help. While his aggressor adjusted his glasses, Art shot a glance at Phil. Phil just shrugged as if to say, "What am I supposed to do?"
"WELL, SNITCH?"
Art snapped to attention. "I don't have it. But I know where it is! It's at the woodpile in Lohsie's woods. I left it there when Phil hurt his leg. We went back looking for it but it was gone. Bauer, I swear I'll buy you a new one."

Bauer twitched with anger. Phil confirmed Art's story but Bauer didn't back off. "I'm gonna get you, you snitch! You'll see. You better get my bat back!" With that he threw Art to the ground. Satisfied that he had made his point, Bauer adjusted his glasses and headed for home.

ART GOES ON A MISSION

Over the following month Bauer had, for some creepy reason, not mentioned the bat at all. He was still being a bully, but Art almost believed that he had gotten over his stupid baseball bat.

Then one day Bauer pulled a fast one. He told everyone to get their baseball mitts and meet at the yard beside Lohsie's woods to play a baseball game called "run-down". But when everyone gathered around, Bauer announced that he couldn't find a ball. So, he said, someone had to go get "Lohsie's stockpile". Old Man Lohsie would pick up any baseballs that he found on his property and stack them into a pyramid on his back porch, almost daring the kids to try and get them.

"Let's take a vote. All those in favor of Art going to get our baseballs back say 'Art!'" Everyone shouted "Art!" Turning away, even Phil mumbled it, knowing he was betraying his best friend. This was no time for loyalty.
"All opposed?"
Art didn't bother to say a word. He'd been duped again.
"You're it, Art... unless you're chicken..."

  Art took one last look at the gang. Some said words of support, but Art knew that once he climbed over the flimsy stretch of fence that ran along the backside of Lohsie's property, he'd be on his own. The others were just glad that they weren't the ones chosen to make the dangerous trip to Lohsie's back porch. It was written all over their dirty faces.

  Tossing Phil his Chicago Cubs baseball cap for safekeeping, Art turned to get a leg-up from Bauer. "Don't forget, if there's a lot over there, stuff 'em down your shirt." Art didn't acknowledge the advice. His thoughts were in a whirlwind and sounds were muffled. After being hoisted up, Art crawled over the fence and dropped to the other side.

UMMPH! His feet stung from the heavy landing. Standing knee deep in high grass, Art suddenly felt very alone. The fence separated him from his friends and safety. Already considering his escape, he eyed the long path around the house. The driveway was open to the street, but he would have to run further than if he made his retreat back over the fence.

Crouching like Batman on the prowl, he planned his invasion. Bauer and the gang were on the side of the fence listening. Art was thinking each step out of his mind. He had to be careful because he was all alone. No one would be there to help if he got *his* leg caught in the woodpile. Bauer's hands and head suddenly appeared on the high fence. "BAWK! BAWK! BAWK! What's the matter Art, you chicken?" On the other side of the fence the gang had made a human pyramid so that Bauer could watch his progress.

Art stayed low to the ground and darted from tree to tree. Stopping for a moment at the woodpile, Art looked back at the fence. Bauer's head still peeked over the fence. "Look for my bat while you're over there." It was at that moment that Art realized how much he disliked Bauer. He always dared kids into doing things, and called them "chicken" if they didn't do his bidding. But nobody ever questioned why *he* never had to get the Frisbee out of the sewer. Why *he* didn't have to go get the baseballs. He told stories to scare the other kids and was nothing but a big bully. In fact, every time a horrible story about Old Man Lohsie would go around the neighborhood, it was Bauer who started it.

Art was tired of Bauer making up stories that scared the other kids. Like the time the gang held Bauer up to Lohsie's window. To hear Bauer tell it, that kitchen looked like Dr. Frankenstein's laboratory complete with saws, axes and blood… lots of blood. Both Phil and Art had many bad dreams about that kitchen. Bauer even claimed to have seen Lohsie's cellar and called it *the torture chamber*.

All thoughts of Bauer stopped as soon as Art's eyes locked onto Lohsie's back porch. It was now or never. There was no sign of the old monster. Art dashed across the open gravel toward the porch. As he got closer he could see the baseballs, five or six of them in all, lying on the top step. Grabbing a ball with his right hand, Art heaved it back over the fence, then another, and another. He could hear Bauer announcing to the gang, "He did it! He made it to the porch! He's on the porch!"

After the last ball was thrown, Art looked all around. There was no sign of the ogre. The dark house was quiet, eerily quiet. His curiosity got the best of him. Cautiously edging further onto the porch, the boy glanced at the driveway. Still feeling safe, he inched his way past the back door and toward the kitchen window. Climbing up onto the railing, Art held onto the gutter for support. His mind raced as he prepared himself for the horrible sight that awaited him.

"Saws, and blood...," Bauer had said a thousand times.

None of the kids had ever seen inside the old kitchen... except for Bauer. The only sound Art could hear was his own heartbeat. Peeking through the break in the old lace curtain, Art's noticed that his hands were trembling. After all, Lohsie could pull his old junker car into the drive at any moment. Glancing back at the driveway Art quietly urged himself to go further. "I've got to see for myself."

Squinting to make out objects, Art pressed his nose and fingertips against the dirty glass. Bauer's voice echoed in the distance but Art paid no attention. Staring, wide-eyed into the window he had two thoughts going through his mind. The first was that Bauer was still shouting loudly. The second was that Art, for the first time in his life, didn't care.

Art was terrified. At least Bauer had his gullible gang of followers for support when he looked through that kitchen window. Art was desperately alone in a place where he didn't belong. His nervous eyes began to twitch. Suddenly, in the blink of his mind's eye, he appeared... Lohsie! Lightning fast reactions sent Art sprawling off the railing and onto the wooden porch. Heart pounding, he looked back up at the window. Lohsie was gone. His mind had played a trick on him. His imagination had gotten the best of him. Without wasting a second, the frazzled boy struggled back to his feet and scampered off the porch to safety.

LOHSIE RETURNS

The old black junker ambled its way around the corner at a snail's pace then turned into the gravel driveway. The engine sputtered and spit, then fell silent. The door's hinges creaked. Old Man Lohsie was home.

His calloused hand fumbled for the key. Putting it up to the keyhole, the old man sensed that something was out of place. Instinctively looking around, Lohsie's cold eyes saw that the pyramid of baseballs was gone. Grumbling aloud, the ogre disappeared into his lair.

CLUB RULES

Art peered up at the tree house for signs of life. Bauer had to be inside. They were supposed to meet there when the streetlights came on. And they had been on for quite some time. The ladder was pulled up so no one could sneak up and listen in. Then he remembered the bell. Giving the rope a jerk, Art was surprised at the racket it made. Not as surprised as Phil and Bauer. Phil's head was mere inches from the bell and its sudden clanging inside the tree house sent him tumbling off of his milk crate chair.

Bauer's head popped out of the tree house. "It's just Art." Dropping the ladder down, Bauer

disappeared back into the tree house. Art gripped
the rungs tightly as he headed for the top.

"I can't stay long, you guys," Art announced as he sat
down on a crate.

"This won't take long. We just have to take a vote on
something." Bauer adjusted his glasses, "Now that
my tree house is finished, we've decided to use it for
our clubhouse. Phil's already in the club 'because his
dad donated the ladder. So Phil's a member. Now
it's your turn, Art. What can you contribute to our
club?"

Art winced. "WE decided?"

If you don't have anything to contribute, like a radio
or walkie-talkies, or somethin' like that, Phil and I will
just have to think of an initiation for you. It's only
fair, Art... and around here I say what's fair."

  It felt like a bomb went off deep in Art's gut. As
usual, he was out numbered two to one. Bauer acted
like he was in deep thought for a moment then came
up with an idea. "Just a second..." Bauer leaned over
and whispered something into Phil's ear, then
giggled.

"O.K., Art. Do you want to be in our club?"
Art stammered, "Yeah, but-"
"Great, then your initiation is to get my baseball bat

back from Old Man Lohsie.   All those in favor of Art getting the bat raise your hand." Bauer and Phil both raised a hand. "That's two out of three, loser."

  Art was furious.
On the way home, Phil admitted that Bauer had planned the whole setup. "You know what I think, Phil? I think Bauer is a hundred times meaner than Mr. Lohsie... and I'm sick of it." Art's teary eyes looked away from Phil for the rest of the walk home.

LOHSIE!

  The next day after supper all the kids in the neighborhood met over on Milton Street to play tap-football. Bauer walked up and immediately took charge. "O.K. you guys, I'll be captain of my team..." "Wow, big surprise." Phil mumbled.

  Grabbing Phil by the shirt Bauer growled, "Got somethin' to say, you rock head?" Phil looked startled. "Well, rock head?" Bauer grabbed him by the hair and threw him to the ground. When Phil said nothing, Bauer sneered, "I didn't think so."

Since Bauer had arrived, the teams could finally be chosen. Bauer was always the captain, and always picked the same kids to be on his team. If anyone thought it was unfair, Bauer would just take out a quarter and flip it. He always won by flipping it, calling "heads", and then putting the quarter back into his pocket before the others could see it.

The game, once started, played well into the evening. One by one, the kids would slowly quit and go home, especially after the streetlights came on.

The "little kids" had to be home when the streetlights came on. Some wouldn't admit that they had to go until their mother or father called for them from across the block. It was better to be in trouble with your parents than to be called a "baby" by Bauer.

It was getting late, but Bauer, Art, and Phil were still playing football catch in the street. Bauer's finger drew the play pattern in the dirt while Phil listened intently, keeping his back turned so that Art couldn't peak. Art waited, more bored than anxious. Out of the corner of his eye he noticed a silhouette in the shadows. While they had innocently been off their guard, Old Man Lohsie had appeared out of the darkness and was walking toward them. Bauer saw him and twitched with fear. Frozen, all three boys were seeing their nightmares come true... Lohsie was coming to get them!

His gigantic figure stepped under the streetlight, casting a spine-tingling shadow that made their hearts race. Then, as the boys stared in disbelief, the ogre raised high above his head... A BASEBALL BAT! Waving it around and shouting at the boys, he took a step toward Art, then turned and looked straight at

Bauer. This is as close as any of them had ever been to Mr. Lohsie'

Bauer was horrified. Lohsie had finally gone berserk and come for them. Art and Phil hoped that Lohsie was out to catch Bauer, but no kid was safe. Bauer had told them that many times. Bauer screamed and disappeared into the shadows. Phil and Art ran in different directions, running as if their lives depended on it.

Having found safety on the other side of a fence, Art peeked back through. Lohsie had stopped chasing them and was just standing there under the streetlight – holding the baseball bat. Art was paralyzed with fear. Lohsie stood motionless for what seemed minutes then turned and started to walk away. Art watched breathlessly as the old man stopped dead in his tracks. His panic proved to be justified when Lohsie turned and, like a wild animal sniffing out its prey, looked toward the fence where Art lay in wait.

Art blinked his eyes, startled, as the ogre approached. Nervously, he looked around for an escape route. He was trapped. Another fence would have to be scaled to get out, and Lohsie would see him for sure if he tried to make a break for it. Closing his eyes firmly, Art prayed to God to make him invisible. Make him disappear. It was his only hope. Slowly his eyes opened, and there, just two feet away, stood Old Man Lohsie. Only the fence stood between Art and certain death.

Art didn't move a muscle. Peeking through the fence he could see the ogre's boots and work trousers. He was so close that Art could hear him breathing. On the other side of the fence Lohsie was listening, too. Art knew that this was the end. He was a dead meat. Numb with fear, he closed his eyes once more.

Art's mother's voice echoed through the night air. His clenched eyelids popped back open. The streetlights were on and she was calling him home for the night. Art didn't dare move a muscle. All he could do was sit quietly, waiting to see what the old man would do next. But when he peeked through the fence... Lohsie was gone. Standing up and peeking over the fence, Art cautiously scanned the area where the ogre had been.

Suddenly, just inches from his face, something whacked the fence hard. Startled, Art fell backward. "MOM!" Just the fact that she left the house wearing her nightgown, cold cream and curlers, told Art that he was in big trouble. The yardstick was just for emphasis.

"Not another word out of you, young man. For crying out loud, it's been dark for an hour and you're not home. For all I knew, you could have been lying in a ditch somewhere..."
Art thought to himself, "I almost was!"

All the way home he suffered swats from the yardstick. By the time they got there, his rear was sore from the thrashing.

INITIATION DAY

Art stayed inside the next morning in hopes that Bauer would forget about the initiation. But midway through the afternoon Art heard a knock at the door. Sure enough, Bauer and Phil had remembered.

On the way over to Lohsie's woods Art started asking questions. "What if he's there? What if I can't find the bat?" Art prayed that the old man had left it on the back porch along with the stray baseballs. Bauer assured him that they would stand guard and warn him if Lohsie came home unexpectedly.

All three boys quickly got to work on a makeshift lean-to to use as cover for Phil and Bauer. Using fallen branches from a nearby tree they positioned them against Lohsie's fence. The knotholes in the fence were perfect for peeking through.

Lohsie's car wasn't in the garage or the driveway, but that only made Art more edgy. He would rather know where the old codger was at all times and have Phil keep an eye on him, but today Lohsie was nowhere to be seen.
"Good luck, Art", Phil whispered as he gave him a leg-

up onto the fence. As soon as Art's feet hit the ground on the other side of the fence, Art ducked and jumped behind a tree. Carefully making his way from tree to tree, he could hear Bauer's voice faintly giving instructions.

Stopping at the woodpile to catch his breath, Art's mind raced. He shouldn't be doing this. He felt something very wrong about it. After all, he *was* trespassing. Signs were posted everywhere. He was risking his life for Bauer's stupid initiation.

Art sprinted to the edge of the gravel driveway and slammed himself against the garage. Looking in, he could see Lohsie's "contraption", as Phil called it. They weren't sure, but they believed that it was what the old man used to dig the big holes in the back yard.

Looking toward the porch, Art realized that there was no turning back. Dashing across the gravel and up the steps, Art lost his balance and his momentum sent him tripping into the screen door. Quickly getting to his feet, Art let out a nervous giggle.

Jumping up on the railing for a better view, Art had the eerie feeling that something, or someone, was watching him. His eyes wandered across the gravel driveway. His pumping heart nearly exploded. There, sitting next to the garage in high grass...was Lohsie's car.

"He's home... Lohsie is HOME!"

Without hesitating, Art jumped back down onto the porch. Landing on all fours, he scurried quickly in an attempt to stand up. It was too late! Towering over him like a mountain stood Old Man Lohsie! The old man was blocking his escape. A calloused mitt of a hand snatched Art up by the scruff of the neck. Looming like a bear with a freshly caught fish, Lohsie turned and carried the screaming child into the house.

Bauer and Phil listened in disbelief, first to Art's screaming, then to the slamming of the screen door. Art was a goner for sure.

Once inside the kitchen, Lohsie loosened his grip. Art twisted himself free and ran behind the kitchen table. His crying was now out of control as he jockeyed to keep the table between himself and the old man. As the terrified child watched carefully, the scary old man turned his back and reached for something in the sink. Art's mind raced as the old man turned...

Art's eyes twitched as he prepared for the worst. His mind raced through horrible images… Lohsie raising a knife… a baseball bat… an axe! Bauer had always told them that Lohsie would get them with an axe!

Art sobbed uncontrollably.

Lohsie took a step toward him and held out his hand. Art realized that it wasn't a knife or a baseball bat. It wasn't even an axe… it was a damp washcloth. Art froze, staring straight into the old man's eyes to see what he was going to do next. Before Art could make a move toward the door, the old man put a hand on his shoulder and began carefully wiping the tears from his puffy, scared little face. Art's sobbing began to calm down as he realized that Mr. Lohsie wasn't going to kill him after all. The damp cloth felt good on his burning face. The old man was trying to *help* him.

Art took the washcloth from him and wiped his whole face, then blew his nose into it. Lohsie carefully took the cloth with two fingers and tossed it into the sink. Then he walked over to the window and pointed at the smudges Art had left while retrieving the baseballs. Nodding his head, Art admitted that he was the one that had been spying in the window. Lohsie's stone face broke into a grin.

Walking to the door, Lohsie motioned toward the steps where the pyramid of baseballs had once been. Nodding, Art sobbed, "We just wanted our baseballs back. Bauer made me do it." Lohsie looked confused. Art watched as the old man put a teapot on the oven. "Bauer's is a bully and said that you'd kill us if you caught us on your property. That's why we always run away. And when I left his baseball bat at your woodpile, he said he'd beat me up if I didn't get it back."

Lohsie thought for a moment. Then without saying a word, walked over to the closet. Opening the door, he reached down and picked up something. Turning around, Lohsie held up Bauer's baseball bat. Art let out a scream so loud that the old man dropped the bat to the floor.

Art fought to catch his breath. The sight of Mr. Lohsie in front of him with the bat was too much for him to handle. Lohsie painfully bent over and picked up the bat. Lohsie's thick, gray hair glistened. His hands were weathered and rough. Holding out the bat once again, Lohsie grumbled a few garbled words and motioned for Art to take it. Slowly Art reached up and took it from his hands.

 What started out as a little rumble in the pit of his stomach, soon erupted into nervous bursts of laughter. Looking up at the old man, Art could see that he was smiling.

"Bauer said you were mean. He said that you killed kids... ha, ha...,"
The old man grinned and shook his head.
Art continued, "You don't do you?"

 Lohsie, shaking his head, motioned for the boy to sit down. Walking through a doorway, Lohsie disappeared from sight. Art considered bolting but was too afraid to make a move. He imagined getting to the back door and WHAM! Lohsie would appear out of thin air! Art looked around the quiet kitchen.

 The old man returned holding a book. Opening it and thumbing through, he found what he was looking for. Placing the book of pictures down on the table, the old man, for the first time to Art, seemed *human*. The photo that Lohsie wanted Art to see was of two boys on a swing set. The picture was old and tattered. In broken English, Lohsie spoke. "Don't be afraid... I had family, boys, like you." Putting his finger on the photo he explained, "Mein Karl und Omar..." Flipping the page he pointed to another black and white photo. It was of the two boys, older, dressed in military uniforms. Posing side by side, the pride and excitement of the moment shown on their faces as the boys waved at the camera. Lohsie, lost in memories, sighed "Karl und Omar..."

Art stood quietly for a moment, finally gathering the courage to ask, "You had kids? But Bauer said you hated kids. He said you killed your wife and buried her in the woods. It was all lies?"

Lohsie nodded his head.

At that moment Art made a grand discovery. Art suddenly saw the man for what he really was. He wasn't a monster who hated kids. Bauer was wrong. Old Man Lohsie wasn't a monster at all... he was just a German man that didn't speak English very well. No wonder the kids couldn't understand him when he yelled at them. Art felt, for the first time in his life, empowered. Bauer's lies and bullying had controlled the neighborhood kids long enough. The truth was clear. Lohsie was just an old man that lived alone, not a monster, not an ogre, just an old man.

And Bauer was just a liar who wore glasses and had a nervous twitch.

The old man wiped a tear from his eye as he closed the photo album. Only then did Art notice the wedding picture on the cover of the book, a young Lohsie kissing his beaming bride.

Years of Bauer's lying and bullying were suddenly washed away. None of it mattered now that Art knew the truth, the truth about Bauer and the truth about Mr. Lohsie. The other kids in the neighborhood would never believe that Old Man Lohsie could be nice. After years of believing the worst about this monster, Art realized that the other kids would just have to learn the truth about Lohsie for themselves. But bad thoughts still lingered, his nervousness about being in the strange kitchen kept him on edge. "I better go now." Art walked toward the door. The old man said nothing, just sat staring at the tattered collection of pictures. Turning back, Art felt the need to say *something*. Slowly he stammered "Can I come back sometime?" The old man stood up, saying nothing.

Art felt uncomfortable, as if something was suddenly wrong… horribly wrong. His mind flashed back to the sight of Lohsie's silhouette under the streetlight. How he stood waving the baseball bat. But this time, in his mind, it wasn't a bat in Lohsie's hands... it was an axe! *Bauer was right all along!* The whistle of the teapot pierced the silence, snapping him from his spine chilling hallucination.

The old man shuffled over to the teapot.

Holding the bat, Art stared for a moment at the steam coming out of the teapot, then at the old man. He looked alone standing in his humble little kitchen. Memories of his wife lay all around him, in the decorative towels at the sink, in the cross stitch flowers that hung, framed, on the wall, and even in the dingy curtains that covered the windows. Little touches that made him feel near her, though she had been gone for many years. Art carefully closed the door behind him and leapt down the porch steps. Resting the bat across his shoulders he walked into Lohsie's woods, unafraid.

IT'S GOOD TO BE KING

The gang wasn't at the fence where he'd left them. They probably ditched at the first signs of trouble. "Some help you guys were." Art thought. Instinctively going from hideout to hideout, he made his way around the block. He wondered how his story would come out when he got back to the gang. Should he tell them the truth, that Bauer was just a lying bully and that the old man they thought was a monster really wouldn't hurt a flea? After all, Bauer had it coming. Years of lying were about to catch up with him.

Art finally found everybody out in the street in front of Mr. Lohsie's house. Bauer had the whole gang busy playing street football when Art got there. The kids immediately shouted, "Alright Art!" and "Way to go!" They wanted to drop their game and run to him, but didn't dare for fear of what Bauer might do. Art held the bat up above his head then let it drop to the ground.

"Here's your stupid bat, Bauer. Now we're even." The gang was proud of Art. Nobody, NOBODY was ever even with Bauer. He would never allow it. But for the moment, all eyes were on Art. Everyone watched except Bauer. He just pretended not to see Art or his bat lying on the ground, and kept shouting at Phil, "Go long, go long… keep going, keep going…" Bauer had no intention of throwing the ball to Phil, but kept urging him on. "Go further!"

Waiting for just the right moment, Bauer suddenly tucked the football into his gut and ran it in for a touchdown. After doing his annoying touchdown dance, Bauer reeled back and spiked the ball into the ground. The kids watched as the ball bounced high into the air.

Lohsie had come out of his front door and was leaning over to check his mailbox when he heard the thud. Standing straight up, or as straight as he could, the old man looked over at the kids. The ball rolled awkwardly up to his front steps. For a moment nobody moved a muscle. Looking over at Bauer, Art challenged, "You spiked it, Bauer, go get it. It's only fair…" The words stung Bauer as he realized that everybody was watching. Phil was in shock. Art was right and Bauer stood speechless for a moment. Bauer's eyes stared Art down. Art took in a deep breath and stood even taller.

Bauer snarled, "Who died and made you king, Art?" Art's confident grin surprised Bauer. Looking to Lohsie, the bully realized that this was no time to argue. Just then, "the ogre" let out a gut wrenching yell that startled everyone. Bauer, Phil and the rest of the gang ran for their lives.

Art watched Bauer run until he was completely out of sight. He wanted to enjoy the moment. Turning around, Art couldn't believe his eyes. Lohsie had put his mail down and was standing, statue of liberty style, with the football. Reeling back, Lohsie let the ball fly.

It fell short of Art, bouncing and rolling, until it finally came to rest at his feet. Art giggled, shouting "Thank you! Mr. Lohsie", as he leaned over to pick up the ball. Lohsie said nothing, just picked up his mail and disappeared into the house.

The curious and excited kids gave Art a hero's welcome. "WAY TO GO, ART! WAY TO GO! You got Bauer's football back!" Phil slapped Art's back in congratulations. The gang huddled around Art so tightly that Bauer had to quietly drift to the back of the group. Phil and Art watched Bauer turn to walk away. "Hey, Bauer...,"Art shouted over the cheers of the crowd. "THINK FAST!" Art threw the football. Bauer caught it, fumbled with his precious baseball bat then adjusted his crooked glasses.

"Bauer!" Art waited until Bauer turned around. "I want you to quit picking on us. And I want everybody to hear you say 'Thanks, Art, for going into Lohsie's woods when I was too scared. I was chicken.' We're tired of you being a bully, so say it." The whole gang watched in disbelief. "It's only fair, Bauer. And around here, WE say what's fair."

Bauer made a quick move to come toward Art but the gang of kids quickly blocked his path. Bauer stopped his advance. Looking from one kid to the next, Bauer hoped to see some sign of support. But it was too late. He had lost his power over them. No one moved a muscle. Bauer thought for a moment, and then to everyone's surprise... he said it. And he said it all, even the part about being a chicken.

Humiliated, Bauer quickly gathered his stuff and ran awkwardly away. The gang laughed and jeered, "Go home, chicken! *BAWK! BAWK! BAWK!*"

The kids watched until he was out of sight before erupting in jubilant celebration. The kids slapped Art on the back and shouted, "You really told him, Art!

That was awesome!" Art stood silently, still shaking from his run-in with Bauer. Looking up, he noticed that the streetlights were on, "Game over, I've got to go home now. Everybody meet at the telephone pole tomorrow morning for some hide and seek."

The gang dispersed, happy that the bully Bauer was no longer calling the shots.

PART TWO - THE NEW KID

"... Eighteen, nineteen, twenty. READY OR NOT HERE I COME!"

On summer days Art and the gang loved to play hide-and-seek. The telephone pole on Milton Street was "home-base" and the whole neighborhood was "inbounds". Only the woods around Old Man Lohsie's house was "out of bounds", every place else was fair game.

The boys ran between houses, climbed trees and hid behind garbage cans while the kid that was "it" closed his eyes and counted to twenty. Whenever a kid made it safely to "home-base" he would shout, "ALI, ALI, IN COME FREE!" Only then would the others crawl out of their hiding places and wander back to base. If they didn't hear the call they could be hidden for hours, not knowing whether it was safe to come out or not.   Other days they played baseball at Hankey's Lot or ran football plays over on Milton Street. These were the exciting days of summer vacation.

Each afternoon the familiar chimes of the ice cream truck caused a panic as children ran home screaming, "Ice cream! The ice cream truck is here!" Parents stood waiting with a handful of change so the kids didn't have to slow down in their race to catch the truck before it got out of sight.

Every evening Art's mother shouted his name from the back porch loud enough for the whole neighborhood to hear, "AR-THUR! It's time for SUP-PER!" The kids would gripe and grumble, not wanting the day to end.   The smell of charcoal and steaks drifted in the air as the kids, one by one, heard their mother's calling them home from across the block.

With only a week left of vacation, these joyous events would come to an end on that most dreaded of days... the first day of school.

FIRST IMPRESSIONS

"Dang it... time out! I've got to tie my shoe again..." Art said, dropping the football to the ground. Phil scooped it up and shuffled over to the curb, "CAR!" The dozen or so kids stepped up onto the curb and watched the moving truck amble by and turn into a driveway. The house had been vacant for months with a "FOR SALE" sign firmly planted in the front yard. Art and Phil didn't disguise their interest as the family, one by one, spilled out of the tall truck.

"They've got a kid...," Phil reported. The group of boys stood silent, not knowing what to make of this new arrival.   "And it looks like, wait, aw man, a GIRL!" The group of boys showed their disgust until they saw the boy crawl out of the truck. "Hey, there's a boy too."

The short, blonde boy stood by his sister as the parents took pictures of them in front of their new home. Art couldn't help but notice that the boy looked different for some reason. The new kids watched the group of boys in the street and the group of boys watched them. The parents noticed the children eyeing each other.
"You can meet your new friends tomorrow, but we need you to stay close to Mommy and Daddy right now. Let's go see your new rooms!"

The group of boys in the street burst out in giggles. A voice from behind the group mocked "Stay close to your Mommy and Daddy..." Phil and Art turned around just as Bauer made his way into the group. "Oh no, Bauer, we've already got teams picked so go pick on somebody else." Phil threw the football to Art and continued, "We're in the middle of a game…" "You just don't want to get embarrassed when-" Suddenly an angry voice interrupted him, "They said they don't want you to play, punk… so take a hike." Brad Bergman, Phil's older brother jogged up to the group. "Phil, Mom wants you to be home when the streetlights come on so she can cut your hair." Turning to Art, Brad shouted "Throw me the ball."

Art, gladly threw the ball to the best football player the neighborhood had ever seen. Brad was much older and played varsity for South Side High. He also played baseball and ran track. He was good at everything. Every kid in the neighborhood wanted to grow up and be a sports star just like Brad. "Phil, run a button hook pattern on ten. Hut, hut, hike!" Phil took off running. Brad reeled back and rifled the ball to Phil. Fumbling for it, Phil pulled it in and started walking back to the group. "No, Phil, you know better than that, show some hustle!" "Okay, I'll be home soon. Just let us play our game, g'yall." Brad, wearing sweats and running shoes, broke into a jog and headed down the street.

Returning to their game, Art noticed that Bauer had walked away. Phil and Art enjoyed playing with the gang when Bauer wasn't around. They had stood up to him as a group, but Phil and Art were still scared of an encounter that might get them beat up. Art knew that Phil could take Bauer if he had to, but Phil didn't know it. He was a little bigger than the other kids, and the only one that stood as tall as Bauer.

They didn't pay attention as the new family moved box after box into their new garage... until they saw the trampoline. The dad was struggling with it when suddenly a dozen kids appeared out of nowhere offering assistance. "Well, that's real nice of you, kids. Just grab a side and we'll walk it into the back yard."
"We saw that you have a kid. Can he come out and play?" Art said, struggling with his side of the trampoline.
"Not today. They've had a big day and we still have things to unpack. Maybe tomorrow you can come back and meet Johnny and Maggie. They would love to have kids to play with so thanks for offering." Art looked at Phil, smiling. "I'm so good. We come back tomorrow and we'll be jumping on a trampoline!" Phil gave Art a high five for his quick thinking.

Once the trampoline was in place, the man thanked the kids for their help. The boys walked away just as the streetlights came on. "I've got to go." Phil said sadly. "Yeah, me too," Art announced. With that, the game ended and the players all went home, anxious for the next day to come so they could go play with the new kids.

TWO WORLDS COLLIDE

Phil's mom shouted, "Good morning Art, you're up early. He'll be right out. He's combing his hair..." Art laughed when Phil came outside because his haircut was so short. "G'yall, Phil, you got a buzz!" The boys razzed each other about everything, especially haircuts. Phil's mom liked to cut it short, but nothing compared to Art's dad. Art's dad made him sit in the middle of the kitchen on a step stool while he sheared him like a sheep. When he was finished there was nothing left to comb, so Art got his share of taunting too. Today it was just Phil's turn.
"Let's go meet the new kid and jump on his trampoline, you want to?" Phil said bluntly. So off they went to see the new neighbors.

Walking up to front door the boys realized that the driveway was empty. Art knocked on the door while Phil rang the doorbell. No response. The boys listened for noise inside the house but heard nothing. "Where could they be?" Phil looked disappointed. Art rang the doorbell again and waited... and waited. "They're not home. We'll have to come back later..." Art walked off the porch and looked around the side of the house. "The gates open... but they're not here."

Phil walked past him and stopped at the gate leading to the back yard. "Aw man, that trampoline *rocks*! Let's go try it out, Art."

"We can't go back there, Phil. Let's come back later." Art said as he peeked through the open gate. "But it does *rock*..."

"Well, what are we waiting' for? C'mon, just for a minute. They're not even home." Phil ran into the yard and jumped up onto the trampoline. It was about fifteen feet across and looked like it belonged at a circus. The new kid must be rich to have something so cool, Art thought.

Phil bounced higher and higher, laughing with excitement. Art heard the truck and a car pull up to the front of the house and warned, "THEY'RE

HOME!!!" Phil bounced off of the trampoline and made a hard landing onto the ground.

Art panicked, "WE'RE TRAPPED! We are so busted..." Phil pulled himself together and urged Art, "Look normal, just follow me." Art tried to calm down and "look normal" as they walked through the gate and into the front yard.

"Well, Johnny, Maggie, look who's here. These boys came over to play, isn't that nice?" The lady leaned over and brushed the boy's hair with her fingers. "You just introduce yourself to these nice boys and don't be shy." Turning to Phil and Art she warned, "You boys will have to excuse Johnny, he's terribly shy. Maybe you kids will help break him out of his shell." Looking back to Johnny she instructed, "Your dad and I will be in and out of the house if you need us. Have fun!"

The adults walked into the house, leaving the four kids standing awkwardly, not knowing what to say. The new kid was younger than Phil and Art, while the sister looked a little older. The girl drifted back to the truck and made herself busy carrying small boxes into the house.

"Hey, you want to check out your trampoline?" Art offered cleverly. The new kid, Johnny, mumbled under his breath.

"My name's Art. This is Phil."

Phil and Art ran right up to the trampoline and climbed on. Bouncing haphazardly into each other and laughing. It wasn't often that they got the chance to jump on a trampoline so they didn't waste any time. The boys were laughing and enjoying themselves when they heard someone crying. Looking down, they saw Johnny bawling his head off and running into the house. "What's wrong with him?" Phil asked innocently.

"I don't know..." Art answered.

Johnny's mom came storming out of the house, pulling the bawling Johnny along by one hand. "You kids let Johnny play. He wants to jump on the trampoline too. You kids take turns and play nice or nobody gets to jump on the trampoline. Only one at a time so nobody gets hurt." Releasing the sobbing boy, she turned and went back into the house.

Art looked at Johnny and asked, "You want to jump for a while?"

Little Johnny sheepishly nodded his head. So Phil and

Art climbed down and let Johnny take their place. Johnny, still sobbing, just stood in the middle of the trampoline.

"Well, jump!" Art shouted, more than a little irritated.

Johnny bounced a little, but never got very high. "Go higher!" Phil shouted. "Higher!" Little Johnny stopped bouncing and climbed down to the ground. Beginning to bawl, he raced toward the house.

"Where is he going now?" Art looked at Phil, "What'd we do?"
"Nothin'! He's just a cry baby, I guess."

Phil jumped back onto the trampoline and started bouncing, trying to get higher and higher with each jump. Art watched the house, wondering what was going on with the new kid. Once again the door swung open, but this time it was Johnny's sister that came out screaming. "If you can't play nice with Johnny than you just go on home."
"But we didn't do anything!" Art said, in shock.
"Well you did something because you scared Johnny. You're bigger than him and should let him play too."
"But he was playing!" Turning away from the girl Art

called out, "Let's go, Phil. This kid's weird. He can play on his trampoline all he wants. We're outta here."

Phil and Art left the cry baby and his big sister and headed out the gate. Johnny's dad was in the front yard and shouted, "You leaving so soon?"
Art tried to explain, "Yeah, Johnny weirded out on us. I don't know what we did, but he keeps running away and crying. We didn't do anything, honest. He had his turn on the trampoline and still started bawling..."

"Don't worry about it boys. He's not used to having friends. He's mentally challenged and acts much younger than he really is. Try to include him as much as you can, though, o.k.? He'd love to play with other kids but most kids don't understand. He's just like everybody else, just a little slower. Making friends is just a little harder for him..."
Art assured him that they would watch out for Johnny and include him when they were out playing.

"That's real nice of you boys and I appreciate it. His mother babies him a little too much, but I guess that's what mothers do. But you boys treat him like any other kid. He'll be going to Abbot Elementary in the Special Ed classes. Where do you boys go to school?"

I go to Abbot but I'm in regular school…" Art answered.

"I go to Zion Lutheran.", Phil added.

"Well, Art, I hope you can keep an eye on Johnny and make him feel welcome at school. You know, help him out if he needs."

"Yes, sir," Art said as he walked away.

Art and Phil were dumbstruck. Phil started laughing, saying, "Art's got a 'special' friend. Art's got a 'special' friend. Are you going to walk to school with him? Are you going to eat at the same lunch table? Will you be in the same class?"

"Shut up!" Art said, punching him on the arm hard. "He'll probably ride the bus."

"Yeah", Phil laughed, "The *short* bus! I didn't know that you were in Special Ed, Art."

"Ha, ha, Phil. You're so funny I forgot to laugh."

Art and Phil weren't bad kids; they'd just never met anyone like Johnny. They didn't know how to act around a mentally challenged person. Art had seen the Special Education students out on the playground at recess. They played many of the same games as the other kids. Some played box ball, others bounced basketballs. But mostly they stayed in a small group, many holding hands, one leading the other so that no one got left behind.

Some were more severe than others. There were the happy ones that constantly broke into laughter when they saw something that excited them. It could be a bird, or a squirrel, anything for that matter. While others sat alone, waiting for someone to tell them what to do next. Art had always seen them from a distance. Meeting Johnny was the first time he actually talked to a "challenged" kid.

JOHNNY MAKES THE TEAM

The next day the kids gathered in the street to play tap football. It was the same as regular football but there was no tackling. As Art and Phil were picking teams, Johnny's dad walked out and addressed the whole group. "Hey guys. I'm Johnny's dad, you can call me Abe. Do you mind if Johnny plays?" Phil and Art looked at each other, not knowing what to say. "You don't have to include him in every play but let him have the ball once in a while." No one said a word until Art offered, "Sure. I guess. Does he want to?"

Johnny's dad said that when Johnny saw them with the football he reacted by clapping his hands. "So, I just thought you could let him in on the fun." Phil blurted out, "Is he going to be a cry baby?" Some of the kids giggled. The adult looked at Phil and admitted, "He may be. He's been pretty good this morning, though, but if he feels scared or uncomfortable he may cry. We'll just have to see, right guys? Just let me know if he's being a problem and I'll take him back in the house."
"O.K., we'll let him try." Art said flatly.

The gang of kids gathered around Art. "Way to go. Now we're stuck with him. You said he could play so he's on your team." The kids stared as Johnny's dad returned with his son. Stopping at the curb, Johnny stepped carefully over it as if it were much higher than it actually was.

"You boys make sure he gets out of the street when cars come, he tends to wander…" Johnny joined Art and Phil, as the other kids blatantly stared at their new neighbor.

Art and Phil helped Johnny along, telling him where to stand, when to run, and when to come back. After a while they slipped back into playing their regular game, letting Johnny go where he wanted, when he wanted. They realized that he knew nothing about football, but Art gave him the ball now and then and the kids shouted encouragement to their new friend. "Go that way! Yeah, keep going. Keep going. TOUCHDOWN! WAIT TO GO JOHNNY! You scored a touchdown!"

"Touchdown! Touchdown!" Johnny shouted, dropping the ball so he could clap his hands. The other kids laughed at him at first, but after a while they realized they were laughing *with* him. They quickly took him under their wing and accepted him into the group. Art felt good when he looked over at Johnny's house and saw little Johnny's mom and dad standing at the window, watching. Abe gave Art thumbs up, while Johnny's mom stood with tears in her eyes. They quickly backed out of sight so that Johnny wouldn't see them.

Johnny only cried once, when he scored a touchdown and didn't want to give the ball back. The other kids lost their patience and wrestled the ball from him to continue playing. Art and Phil calmed him down so that he wouldn't go home unhappy. Finally the kids broke up the game and walked Johnny back to his house. His beaming parents were at the door as Johnny excitedly clapped his hands and shouted "Touchdown... touchdown!"

AN OFFER THEY CAN'T REFUSE

 Johnny's mom came outside and stopped Phil and Art as they were crossing the street. "Wait a second boys, I have something for you." Phil looked at Art and wondered what it could be. Art looked equally interested. "I haven't introduced myself boys, my name is Mary, or Mrs. Alton, which ever you want to call me. You boys were so nice to our Johnny that I wanted to give you this." Reaching out her hand she held out two five dollar bills. Handing one to each of the boys she gushed about how she hadn't seen Johnny so excited in a long time. Thanking the boys again she said, "If there's ever anything that you need or anything that Abe and I can do for you, you just let us know. You promise?"

Art and Phil were so surprised that they didn't know what to say. Finally Art found the words, "Thank you, Mrs. Alton." Phil joined in, "Yeah, thanks!" Mrs. Alton left the boys standing, looking at their new found money. Turning around, she shouted once more, "Remember, if you need anything, you know where we live."

Phil reminded Art about the trampoline; maybe she would let them play on it for a while. Art stopped him short, saying that she'd already been too nice. Art kind of felt guilty about taking the money because Johnny really wasn't that bad. Phil disagreed. "She gives out money! All we have to do is let him play with us a couple of times a week and we can go to the little store and buy all the candy we want!"

"I guess so, but it doesn't seem right…" Art put the money in his pocket and headed for home. Phil shouted after him, "Let's go to the little store after we eat lunch. You want to?" Art didn't answer, he just kept walking.

"Think about it, Art, he can make us money. Just by playing with him we can make money!"

Phil got to thinking about the money on his way home and still couldn't believe his good fortune. He

mentioned it to his mother and she blew her top.
"You march right back over there and you return that
money!
"But mom…"
"No buts. Go right now!"

Phil stomped out of the house, angry at his mom
for ruining everything. As he got closer to Johnny's
house he started to have second thoughts. His mom
didn't know the Alton's. *How would she know if I
returned the money? She wouldn't.* So he convinced
himself that the money was rightfully his. After all,
Mrs. Alton *did* offer it to him. And Art took it too.
That was the last straw. If Art got to keep his money
than Phil decided that he was going to keep his.

Walking past Johnny's house he pulled the five
dollar bill out of his pocket. Glancing down at it, he
turned his attention to the house. Stopping
momentarily, he stuffed the money into his pocket
and headed for home. Picking up the pace, he
started to whistle. He had only learned how to
whistle a few weeks back, so the sound was music
only to him. His mind left the issue of the money and
devoted itself to his new found skill.

Later that afternoon Phil went over to Art's house to play. Once again he suggested that they go up to the little store and buy some candy and an Orange Crush. Art said that he would rather stay home. "Are you crazy, Art? We have money! Let's go spend it!" Phil couldn't contain his excitement. "Maybe we should go back and see if Johnny wants to play. Then we'll have ten dollars each! C'mon, Art, let's go!"

"Phil, I don't think it's right that we take the lady's money for playing with Johnny. He's not that bad. We shouldn't take money for being his friend. You go and spend the money but I'm not going too." Art was proud that he stood up for what was right, even if Phil didn't understand.

"But Art, you took the money…"

"I know, and I shouldn't have."

"Can I tell you a secret? You've got to swear you won't tell anybody." Phil said looking serious.

"I swear I won't tell." Art agreed.

Phil lowered his voice to a whisper, "My mom told me to take the money back… but I didn't."

Art thought about it for a minute and warned Phil, "You're going to be in trouble. You know she's going to find out…"

The boys took their money out of their pockets and

admired it. Art suddenly had an idea. "Hey, wait! We don't have to get in trouble and we don't have to feel guilty! I've got a plan." Thinking for a moment, Art formulated his plan then asked, "Did your dad put a new chain on your bike?"

Phil looked puzzled, "Yeah, why?"

"Alright, I've got to go home now and do chores or I'll get grounded. But I'll meet you at the little store tomorrow morning at ten o'clock."

"Okay. But I thought you didn't want to buy any candy." Phil tried to understand. "You'll see, just bring the money and meet me at the store."

A GIFT FOR JOHNNY

   The next day Art waited for Phil at the little store… and waited. Finally Phil rolled up on his bike and threw it down next to the bike rack. Racing into the store he found Art waiting at the counter.

"I thought you got grounded or somethin'. What took you so long?" Art snapped.

"Whatever, I'm here aren't I?" Phil snapped right back.

"Give me your money." Art demanded.

"What for...?" Phil shot back.

Art picked up a football off of the counter. "...for Johnny."

Phil stared at the ball for a moment, "For Johnny?"

Art grinned with pride, "For Johnny."

Phil put his head down for a moment then looked over at the candy aisle. Shelves of Snicker's Bars, Marathon Bars, Milk Duds and gum, taffy and licorice, it was all *right there*. He took a step toward it as if drawn by a giant magnet. Without looking at Art he asked, "How much is the football?"

Art answered, "Nine dollars." Phil looked at the football and knew he had a decision to make.

A VISIT TO JOHNNY'S HOUSE

Mrs. Alton opened the door and nearly shouted, "Look who's here! Come on in. Johnny is going to be so thrilled!" Leading them through the living room full of furniture that partially blocked the door, Mrs. Alton explained, "Sorry about the mess, boys, but we haven't gotten to set up our room arrangements yet. There's so much to do! Unpack towels and things for the bathroom and the kitchen, we haven't even thought about the furniture. I could just scream. It's never ending!"

Turning the corner and entering another room full of boxes, the boys got their first glimpse of Johnny in his own environment. Sitting at a card table, alone, was Johnny... playing with Blocks? Phil looked at Art. They were both thinking the same thing, *blocks!* It was weird to see a kid that old playing with blocks, but the boys kept their mouths shut. Johnny didn't look up, too lost in his own world to notice their arrival.

"Johnny, your new friends are here! Honey, look at your friends, they came to see you!" His mom was obviously excited, saying, "I've always wanted to say that! Now if you boys behave I'll leave you alone." Phil couldn't stop staring at the blocks on the table. Johnny was almost their age and was still playing with *blocks!*

Stepping forward Art spoke in a louder than usual voice, "Hi Johnny, we brought you something." Mrs. Alton had started to leave the room but turned around to look. Art continued on, "It's a football. We just thought that, well, you're one of the guys, and well, here." Art put the football on the table next to the blocks. Johnny's eyes lit up as he realized that it was his. Still seated, Johnny screamed, "Football! Football!" His excitement boiled over as he clapped his hands and bounced in his chair.

Phil blurted out, "If you don't like it we can take it back." Art glared at him. Mrs. Alton ran up to Johnny and said, "Isn't that sweet, Johnny? They're giving you a football! And it looks new, your very own football! Looking at Art she exclaimed, "He's never had his own football. You boys didn't have to do that!" Phil once again blurted, "If he doesn't like it we can take it back."

Johnny jumped up and threw his arms around Art in a giant bear hug. Startled, Art looked at Mrs. Alton. She chimed in, "Easy, Johnny! You don't know your own strength sometimes. You be gentle! I'm sorry boys but he does love to hug."

Art stepped back, shaken. "Oh, that's okay. Well, we've got to go." Phil laughed openly as they raced for the door. Mrs. Alton shouted after them, "Come back when you can play for a while and we'll have a pizza party!

The boys talked about Johnny a lot over the next few days. Innocently wondering how he became the way he was, what it was like, and if he knew how "uncool" it was to still be playing with blocks. Art knew that when it came time to go back to school he would take a lot of harassment about being friends with Johnny. He acted like he didn't care, but deep down, he was a little embarrassed. Kids can be cruel and Art knew that they wouldn't miss a chance to make fun of him if he was seen goofing around with "the slow kid."

THE BLOCK PARTY

The neighborhood parents got together and thought it would be fun to have a block party to celebrate the end of summer. Preparations were made and tables were set up along the side walk. The street was blocked off with barricades so that neighbors could wander here and there, visiting and laughing with neighbors that they didn't normally get to see. It seemed that everyone on the block showed up, everyone except Old Man Lohsie. He had lived in his rundown house for as long as anyone could remember, but none of the parents knew him. In fact, they told the kids to stay away from Lohsie's woods and "just leave him alone".

Phil's mom met Mrs. Alton and immediately welcomed her to the neighborhood. They chatted about the agony of moving into a new home. Mrs. Alton exclaimed, "There is just so much to do! This house is a little smaller than our old house so we're going to have to have a yard sale. The kids are growing so fast that it's time to let go of all of the baby clothes and furniture. I just want to keep them that age forever but I know that isn't possible. Is it okay to have a yard sale in this neighborhood? Mrs. Bergman assured her, "Oh yes, and don't you worry, if you need any help with it I'd be glad to help you." Looking across the street she noticed Mrs. Carlson and Art, "Barbara, over here! There's someone I want you to meet..."

Mrs. Carlson walked across the street, leaving Art standing on the sidewalk. Phil ran over to him in a panic. "They've been talking and looking over at me. I think my mom knows that I didn't return the money. Art, so help me, if I'm in trouble you owe me five dollars. My mom's going to make me give it back and, oh, I'm so busted..." Art started to worry because the three mothers were now talking to each other. "Yep...we are busted. I'm not supposed to take money either."

Mrs. Alton was excited to make friends with the other mothers..."My Maggie and Johnny are in the house. Maggie is disappointed that she hasn't seen any little girls on the block. And Johnny, well, he's just Johnny. I guess they're still a little shy but I'll make them come out so they can meet everyone in a little while. Which ones are yours?" Mrs. Alton asked as she looked at a small group of kids. Mrs. Bergman pointed, "The taller red head on the sidewalk, that's my Phillip." "And my Arthur is standing next to him. Oh, he'd throttle me if he heard me say that, he hates it when I call him Arthur. Everyone just calls him Art."

Mrs. Alton's face lit up. "Oh, let me tell you, they are very sweet boys." The other mom's looked surprised. She continued, "They've already met the kids. I think that they've really taken to Johnny. Did they tell you about my Johnny?"

Over on the sidewalk, Phil and Art were watching as an adult set up a charcoal grill. Bauer came walking up with a pogo stick. "What'cha doin' girls?"
Art sighed, "Oh, great..." Both boys mustered up and

unenthusiastic "Hey, Bauer."

"You wanna see who can go the longest?" Bauer said, holding out the pogo stick. "I'll go first..." As usual, Bauer took control of the activity and started bouncing up and down on the pogo stick. He bounced a few times and then came down with one foot landing solidly on the ground. Art reached his hand out, "Okay, it's my turn."

"Nuh-uh, I'm not done yet. This time it's for real." Phil and Art started to walk away and Bauer shouted after them, "Don't you want to try it? I know you do!" Art shouted back, "No, you cheater!"

The boys left him there, alone, bouncing on his pogo stick. Still trying to get their attention, Bauer counted loudly, "One, two, three, four, five." Faltering, he quickly gathered himself and started over, "One, two, three, four, five, six." Once again faltering, he shouted so that all could hear, "SIX! IT'S A NEW RECORD!"

Bauer was used to playing alone. He was such a bully that most kids stayed away from him completely. Phil and Art were the only kids in the neighborhood that had been inside his house. Once in a while they would ask him where his dad was and the answer was always the same. "He's golfing at the country club. He's too important to hang around the losers in this neighborhood." Art knew that it was a lie but never exposed the truth.

Art had once heard his parents talking about the money troubles that the Bauer's had. They figured that there was a lot more to the story but didn't pry. Bauer himself had every toy imaginable, but his house was in a constant state of disrepair. The grass grew high around a broken down car that sat beside their garage. Art's dad once complained about Bauer's dad, "He manages to make it to work every day as a mechanic, but he can't seem to fix that car or start his own lawn mower. He needs to put down that bottle and –" Art's mom shushed him before he could say any more in front of young Art.

Someone shouted, "The burgers and hotdogs are done. COME AND GET IT!" All the kids in the neighborhood raced over and crowded around the grill. The chef shouted, "Easy now, form a line, there's plenty for everyone."

Art and Phil's moms were waiting for them when they got to the food line. "What are we going to do with you two?" Art and Phil looked at each other. "What do you mean?" Phil asked cautiously. Art's mom spilled the beans, "You bought that new boy a present. We're just so proud of you both." Art argued, "It wasn't a present, mom, it was a football." Phil looked at his mother to see what she thought. "You little sneak." she said. "That was very nice of you and I'm proud. You're getting to be more and more like your big brother every day!"

Phil and Art ran off as soon as they got their hotdogs. "I told you so. I told you so.", Art shouted into Phil's ear.
"Told me what?" Phil asked.
Art ranted on, "I told you that we should do the right thing and not keep the money!"

They saw little Johnny and his sister sitting at a table all alone. Maggie looked unhappy, scanning the crowd for kids her own age. Johnny sat smiling, rolling his football back and forth across the top of the table.

Art looked at Phil and suggested, "Let's go eat with Johnny. You want to?"
"I guess, but he'd better not hug me or touch my food." Phil stated firmly.

Sitting down at the table the kids awkwardly started a conversation. Maggie seemed to look down on the boys because she was older, but occasionally answered questions with a short "yes" and "no" to keep the conversation going.

  Johnny seemed to be oblivious of the boys as he sat clutching his new football. Art finally got him to answer short questions like, "Are you having fun?" and "Aren't you going to eat?" Johnny said that he had already eaten a hotdog. Art teased, saying "Johnny, you didn't eat it all, you spilled some on your shirt right here..." Pointing to a spot on Johnny's chest Art said, "Right here, see?" Johnny looked down to see the spot just as Art moved his hand up and tapped him on the forehead. Johnny laughed and laughed.

"I got you! Didn't I, Johnny? I got you good!" Johnny squealed and shouted, "You got me! You got me. You're funny." Johnny's sister finally smiled and said, "You better watch it 'cause Johnny will get you back."

"Really, he likes to play jokes on people too?" Art asked Maggie.

"Oh, yeah, he loves to pull pranks on people." Maggie said smiling at Art.   Sliding closer to Maggie on the bench, Art whispered into her ear. She said, "Oh, he'd like that..." She got up and whispered into Johnny's ear.

Johnny started laughing as he reached over and picked up the hotdog off of Phil's plate. Phil screamed out in terror, "Hey, that's mine!" Johnny got up and taunted, "I've got it. It's mine!" Taking a bite out of it, he continued talking with his mouth full, "It's mine now."

Phil looked on in disgust until he heard Art and Maggie laughing.
"You guys... you put him up to that!" Phil said, relaxing a bit. Art whispered something else into Maggie's ear. Maggie recoiled, "No, you tell him." Art got up and whispered into Johnny's ear. Johnny listened intently and broke into a smile, "Give me a hug, Phil. Give me a hug!" Phil jumped up and started running around the table. Johnny, laughing, chased him round and round, shouting, "Hugs for Johnny... hugs for Johnny!"

The adults looked on and laughed, just happy to see the kids having fun. Art and Maggie shared a brief glance. Art realized that he couldn't stop looking at this new girl. Maggie stood up and told Art, "I'll go get your friend another hot dog." Art nearly shouted,

"I'll go with you" then nonchalantly added, "I've got to get another hot dog anyway."

   The adults at the block party with children started to pack things up when the streetlights came on, hoping that the tired kids would go straight to bed when they returned home. Some of the adults stayed out, talking and laughing loudly well into the night. Bauer was the only kid that didn't get called home, so he got to stay out later than all of the other kids. Art's mom always said that Art should be glad that he had parents that loved him enough to give him rules. "The Bauer boy doesn't have it as good as you do.", she often said. But thinking of all the cool stuff that Bauer had, Art found that hard to believe.

BAUER TRICKS ART

   The dreaded day was fast approaching. Before long they would be back in school, getting homework and taking tests. Art didn't dislike going to school, he just loved summer vacation more. The boys talked about the schools they were going to and all of the nerds that went there. Phil was glad that he didn't go to the same school as Bauer. Art wasn't so lucky.

Phil and Art were throwing rocks at a garbage can when Bauer walked up. "Hey, punks, whatcha doin'?" "What does it look like we're doing'?" Art fired back. Disregarding the comment Bauer launched into a speech. "My mom is taking me to Cedar Point tomorrow so I can ride the roller coasters and water rides. It's gonna be awesome. She said I can invite one of you losers to come, but I can only take one. So who wants to go to Cedar Point?" Phil and Art both showed signs of interest but tried to play it down. "I do, I guess." Art said unconvincingly. "I do," Phil said competitively.

As if telling a riddle Bauer urged, "Now remember, I can only take one of you. So I'll have to give you a test to see who should go."
"Okay." agreed Phil.
"Whatever.", added Art."
Bauer launched into his scheme, "Art, I can eat three hotdogs. Can you eat three hotdogs?"
Art responded, "Yeah, I can eat at least three hotdogs."
"I like pizza so much I can eat three pieces of a large without getting sick. Can you top that?" Getting

competitive Art took the challenge, "I can eat a whole pizza! Yeah. I've done it before." Bauer, grinning from ear to ear, slapped Phil on the shoulder, "Well, I've got to pick Phil, because if I took you it would cost my mom too much money to pay for your food. Sorry Art, maybe next year."

Art just closed his eyes. Bauer had tricked him again. Phil jumped up and down, "Awesome, Bauer! Thanks! I've got to go ask my mom if I can go." Running off, Phil didn't even realize the cruel trick that was just played on Art. All he knew was that he was going to ride a rollercoaster!

HANGIN' OUT AT JOHNNY'S

The next morning Art didn't say a word at breakfast. His mother noticed and wondered what could be wrong. "Is everything okay, Arthur?" she said as she walked into the laundry room. The usually chatty boy just sat stirring his Fruit Loops until they got soggy. "What are you and Phillip doing today?" she shouted from the laundry room.

"Oh, probably nothing'... Phil won't be home today, he's going to Cedar Point."

"Oh, that sounds fun. He didn't invite you?" she shouted back.

Art stared into his cereal, "No. He's going' with Bauer."

Mrs. Carlson came into the kitchen with a load of clothes, "Bauer! I didn't know you kids still played with him."

"We don't," Art mumbled, "'cause he's still a big fat bully."

Mrs. Carlson put the basket on a chair, "Now, Arthur, you don't call anybody 'fat', do you hear me?" Art just mumbled, "Yes, mam."

Changing the subject, Mrs. Carlson tossed two shirts to Art. One was red, the other was blue. "I got you these, go ahead and try them on. I want to see you in something other than that tee-shirt." Art grabbed the blue shirt and tried it on. Standing up proudly, he awaited her approval. Art's mom looked at him, disappointed, "What, you don't like the red one?"

"No. I mean yes..."

Arts mom pursed her lips, pouting, "I try to keep you in nice clothes and this is the thanks I get." Picking up the red shirt and throwing it into a basket she snapped, "Here, I'll just take this shirt back or give it to a boy that will appreciate it." Art was confused, but just continued eating breakfast. After a few moments of silence Art finally said, "There's nothing' to do."

Putting down a shirt, Mrs. Carlson disagreed, "That's not true. You can clean-up your room or help me with laundry. I could find something for you to do. Why don't you go visit Johnny? I'm sure that it would mean a lot to him. You just said you don't have anything else to do."

Art thought it over and said, "Maybe I will."
"Maybe you will what? Go clean-up your room?" Mrs. Carlson joked.
"NO!" Art shot back, "Go visit Johnny!"

Art rode to Johnny's house and let his bike fall to the ground. Maggie came to the door and opened it, saying, "I'm glad you're here." Art's heart raced. *She's glad I'm here! She likes me! She likes me!* Suddenly he became very nervous but didn't know why. *Do I like her? Oh my gosh! I've got a crush on her! Keep your cool, Art. Keep your cool! Don't say anything stupid...* She held the door open as he brushed by her. He could smell her hair. "Your hair smells!" he blurted. She tilted her head to the side, "Well, you're weird..." Trying to salvage the situation Art fumbled for words, "I mean it smells girly." "That's good because I *am* a girl!"

Art realized that his best bet was to keep his mouth shut. *Way to go, Art. She thinks you're weird.* Maggie walked him into the living room and continued on, "I'm glad you're here because Johnny is driving me nuts! He's all excited and wants me to sit down and draw with him. I've got better things to do than just sit around the house and draw stupid pictures!"
"Like what?" Art asked, interested.
"I don't know! Anything but babysit him. That's all I am around here, a babysitter for him!" Art didn't know what to say and for a moment just stared at her. Finally he snapped out of his gaze enough to say, "I'm here to draw with Johnny, so you don't have to go nuts." Maggie looked at him with a glowing smile that made Art blush. "You're really going to hang out a while?"
Art fumbled for words, "If you want me to, I mean, if

it will help you. I mean, and I want to, really."
"Come on in. He's in the play room."

  Grabbing Art's hand, she led him through the
house. *She's holding my hand! I'm holding a girl's
hand. The guys can never hear about this.* Entering
the play room Art could see Johnny sitting at a card
table with crayon in hand, drawing.
"Johnny, Art's here. He wants to draw too, isn't that
cool." Johnny didn't look up but grabbed some
crayons and put them down on the table in front of
an empty chair and shouted "Crayons for Art."
Maggie let go of Art's hand and urged him, "Just sit
down and start drawing. He'll be quiet at first, but he
might open up when he feels more comfortable."

  Art sat down and looked at Johnny. His tongue
stuck out as he diligently worked at his masterpiece.
Looking at the picture, Art saw what Johnny had been
working on for over an hour. There was a group of
stick people with their "hands" together, while
another one stood off in the distance. "Johnny,
that's nice. Are they praying?" Art said loudly.
Johnny looked up with a confused look then quickly
drew an oblong circle. As he pointed at the circle he
explained, "Football," then threw his hands in the air

and shouted "TOUCH DOWN FOR JOHNNY! TOUCH DOWN FOR JOHNNY!"

Suddenly swept up in Johnny's simple world, Art couldn't help but smile and laugh along with him. Art took a crayon and touched it to Johnny's picture, "Can I add to it?" Johnny shook his head up and down.

Art drew a goal post next to Johnny in the picture. "This is the goal post for your touchdown." Johnny laughed and laughed. Excited, he put crayon to paper again and added another stickman next to his own. "Who's that?" Art wondered aloud. Proudly pointing at the new figure Johnny answered, "My friend!" Art complimented him saying, "That's good. What's your friend's name?" Johnny looked down and, with his tongue out and a look of determination, scrawled the letters A – R – T.

Art was suddenly glad that he didn't get picked to go to Cedar Point. No rollercoaster could be as awesome as the proud look on Johnny's face. "That's right, buddy. We're friends... give me five!" Johnny slapped Art's upturned hand, smiling from ear to ear.

From the other room Maggie's voice boomed out in laughter. She was on the phone, enjoying a few moments of just being a kid again. She missed her girlfriends from the old neighborhood, but had been too busy helping in the move and watching Johnny to give them a call.

The boys sat for several hours drawing everything under the sun. Art would draw a mountain, and Johnny would add the sun. Then Art would add snow to the mountain, and Johnny would add a football. They laughed so loud that Maggie would stick her head out of the kitchen to say, "You guys are crazy!"

Johnny would shout out, "No girls allowed!" Art joined in, "Yeah, no girls allowed!" Maggie would just shake her head as she disappeared back into the kitchen. The boys had so much fun that Art didn't realize the time. They didn't notice the doorbell's ringing, so it was a surprise when Art's mom walked into the room. "MOM! What are you doing here?"

Maggie stood watching, so Art was embarrassed by the surprise visit. "I just wanted to make sure that you hadn't forgotten where you lived. It's time for lunch." Turning to Maggie, she added, "He'd lose his head if it weren't attached to him." *Way to go mom! Now she thinks I'm stupid! I'm so embarrassed!*

Maggie smiled and left the room. Art's heart sunk, but looking at Johnny reminded him of what was important. It wasn't about Art; it was about his new friend Johnny. *If Maggie doesn't like me that's her tough luck!*

"I've got to go Johnny. It's been fun. Give me five!" Johnny slapped his hand and laughed. As Art and his mom walked to the door he heard Maggie's voice behind him. "Give me five!" she said with her hand up. Art slapped her hand. When Art's mom turned away, Maggie slipped a note to Art and ran away.

Art couldn't wait to read it but waited until he got home. Running to his room and closing the door he quickly took out the note. Taking a deep breath, Art read the three simple words that would change his life forever... YOU'RE MY HERO. He couldn't believe his eyes, "Her hero, I'm her hero!" Realizing that the note was folded, he opened it completely. What he saw made him jump with joy, at the bottom of the page were the letters XOXO!

Carefully folding the note and putting it in his pocket, he bound down the stairs to eat lunch. Smiling far too much, his mother noticed and inquired, "You look like you're up to something today, what's with the big smile?" Holding back, Art just said, "Oh, nothing'," but inside he was screaming, *"MAGGIE ALTON LIKES ME!"*

SHOWDOWN AT JOHNNY'S

The phone rang and Mrs. Bergman had a good idea who was calling. She felt bad because for the third day in a row she had to tell him, "Phillip's not here. I'm sorry, Art, but if he's not with you he's probably down playing at the Bauer's. Go down there, honey, they're probably climbing that darned tree again." "Okay, thank you... bye." Hanging up the phone was hard for Art because he felt like he was losing his best friend.

Ever since they went to Cedar Point Bauer and Phil were best buddies. It was hard not to feel left out when they were off climbing trees and didn't even invite him. *Who needs them? There are plenty of other kids on the block to play with.*

Art started to walk down to the alley heading for Daniel Whistler's house. Daniel wasn't very cool but he did have a pitch-back net. The last time Art played over there he got so good at throwing a baseball at the net that it came all the way back. He could actually catch balls that he threw to himself. Daniel didn't even have to play.

Somewhere along the way, Art changed his path and walked straight to Johnny and Maggie's house. Once again he found Johnny at the card table. This time he had plate of food in front of him. The bib around his neck reminded Art that Johnny was "special". Holding up a bowl Johnny announced, "I'm eating Pudding!"
"You sure are!" Art noticed that his plate of food hadn't been touched. "Aren't you eating any of this? It looks good." Johnny shook his head back and forth and said, "NO!"

Mrs. Alton shouted from another room. "He needs to eat his broccoli before he eats his Pudding..." Johnny had the Pudding all over his shirt and quickly put the bowl down as his mother entered the room. "Johnny, are you eating your chicken and broccoli?" Johnny grinned and said emphatically, "Yes!"

Art was impressed. His new friend probably couldn't tie his own shoes but he could lie just like any other kid. His mom didn't believe him but played along, "Good. Because you know that the Pudding is your reward for cleaning off your plate. Don't you?" "Yes!" he enthusiastically agreed.

As soon as she left the room Johnny picked up his bowl of Pudding and tilted it up to his mouth. Slurping it down quickly, he raced to put the bowl down before his mother returned. Art just had to laugh. Johnny broke a devilish grin and joined in the laughter.

Mrs. Alton came back into the room with a bowl of Pudding for Art. Johnny reached out for it but his mom warned, "You've had enough. You're still in trouble, young man, and you're not getting up from that table until you finish what's on your plate."

As she breezed out of the room she shouted, "He had a tantrum on the trampoline so it's off limits for one more hour. He's got to learn to control his temper!" As soon as she turned her back, Art traded bowls with Johnny. While Johnny slurped up the Pudding, Art kept an eye on the door. "You can't play on the trampoline, for how long?" Johnny was too busy eating to answer. "Dang, Johnny, you're a pig!" Johnny laughed and laughed, "I'm a pig, oink-oink!"

Art was disappointed about the trampoline being off limits, but it didn't seem to bother Johnny. He didn't seem angry that he couldn't go out and play. He was fine with staying in because he seemed to enjoy everything he did. Eating Pudding was a party to him. When other kids were outside playing games and goofing off with friends, Johnny sat at his card table and entertained himself.

Sometimes he got mad, but his tantrums were spontaneous and ended just as quickly as they started. But when he calmed down, he even laughed at himself for crying.

"They're right in here…" Mrs. Alton said, entering the room again. Phil and Bauer trailed her in and started laughing right away. As soon as Johnny's mom left the room Bauer blurted, "I wanted to see your new friend, Art. Phil told me all about him." Art stood up and demanded, "You better get out of here, Bauer. I'm not kidding." "Woo, I'm really scared." Looking at Johnny, Bauer asked rudely, "Are you really mentally retarded?"
"SHUT UP, BAUER!" Art shouted, ready to fight. But before he could say anything more, Johnny's voice

chimed in, "I'm a special gift from God. My mom said that everybody is different, but I'm special…"

Bauer stared for a moment and then got to the point. "Ask him if we can go play on the trampoline." Art laughed, "He's right here and he's not deaf, Bauer. Ask him yourself."
Bauer looked at Johnny, "Hey, 'tardo, can I jump on the trampoline?" Art was embarrassed for Johnny and looked to see his response. Johnny looked up; his bib covered with food, and said, "I'll tell you a secret."
Bauer stepped forward, "What'd he say?"
Art explained, "He wants to tell you a secret. Let him tell you his secret…" Bauer leaned over so that Johnny could whisper into his ear. Art grinned and coaxed Johnny, "Go on, Johnny, tell him a secret." Johnny got close to Bauer's ear and shouted at the top of his lungs, "NO WAY, JOSE!" Bauer jumped back, startled half to death. Johnny and Art burst out laughing. Phil started to laugh but thought better of it. Bauer blew up, "Come on Phil, let's leave these losers and go and do something fun."

Looking at Art he lashed out, "We're gonna go climb my tree and throw apples at stuff. You gonna stay here with him?"

There was a time when Art would jump at the chance to climb that tree. But not today, he sat down at the table with Johnny and stole a piece of his broccoli. "Yes I am. Go climb your stupid tree. I'm going to hang out with my friend." Johnny sat smiling, bursting with pride.

SUMMER'S END

The last day of summer vacation came too soon. Art went over to the Alton's hoping to catch a glimpse of Maggie, but she didn't go out of her way to talk to him. He didn't understand it, but then again, she was a girl. He still had the note hidden in his top secret hiding spot. He would read it once in a while and remember the day that she held his hand and wrote YOU'RE MY HERO XOXO. Art knew that she was a couple of years older than he was, but in his mind, he still wished that she liked him. He tried to hide it but his little heart was broken. It was only puppy love, but it was real to the puppy.

That evening Art had trouble falling asleep. He thought about how fun the summer had been, and how everything was going to change. It would be early to bed, no more staying out until the streetlights came on, and no more ice cream truck. There would be schoolwork, tests and new activities.

He'd learned a lot over the summer. He learned that confidence comes from doing what was right, even if he got bullied for it. Art's mom wanted him to "stay that innocent age forever", but meeting the new kid and his sister had opened Art's eyes to the world as it really was... at times sad and heartbreaking, at times hilarious and carefree. The new kid taught Art that everything was to be appreciated, and nothing to be taken for granted. Everyone was different... but some people were truly special.

PART THREE - MAGIC AT BIG TONY'S

Art and Phil walked nervously to the small shop at the corner of McKinnie and Hanna streets. The old McKinnie Pizza shop had stood vacant for over a year when a new sign appeared in the window, *Coming Soon – BIG TONY'S PIZZA*, a simple sign that stirred interest in the new restaurant and its mysterious owner. Bauer, the bully, had told the guys that Big Tony was a real life giant. In disbelief, Art and Phil wanted to see the Giant with their own eyes.

The bell on the door rang as the boys entered the small shop. On the wall was painted four different sizes of pizza. The largest was about the size of a wagon wheel and labeled Big Tony's Snack. The boys looked at each other in disbelief. There was a long counter that ran the length of the shop ending at the cash register. As the boys stepped up to the counter, a voice shouted from the back "Be there in a fortnight!" Just as quickly, the man bounded out from the back, pulling on little plastic gloves. "Just having you on, lads, what can I get for you?"

Art pointed at the Orange Crush can that was on the counter. Phil meekly said, "One for me too, please." "You want that, an Orange Crush? Well, I'll have to see some form of I.D. Do you have your driver's license, or a passport with a photo? Are you lads old enough to handle that?" Art and Phil stood, frozen with disbelief. This funny sounding man must have been ten feet tall. "What's the matter, cat got your tongue? 'Cause if he has, we'll have to start looking for it, won't we?"

Art asked boldly, "Are you a Giant?"

The tall man laughed, "A Giant, me? Oh, right, I am looking down on you now, aren't I? Well, I'm a Giant until you pay me. Then I'm just like any other bloke. You'll see. You lads go down to the till. Go on, I'm going to show you a magic trick." The boys looked confused.

"Go ahead, to the till. Go on now, go down and stand in front of the cash register and close your eyes." The boys, feeling uneasy, slowly did as they were told.

"Now, keep your eyes closed and turnaround the other way, I can't have you peeking and ruining my magic trick."

On his side of the counter, the tall man walked toward the "till". As he got there, he stepped down two steps and stood at the register. "Alright, lads, open up. You can turn around now. The magic's all done."

The boys swung around and gasped at what they saw. "How did you do that? You're not really a Giant..."

"Ah, but I am if you want to believe I am, lads. Now, go on, take your drinks and go. I have a lot of, you know, "giant" things to do. I've got to make a couple of pies and then I'm off to slay a Cyclops and what not. Now, off you go."

  The boys grabbed their change and raced out the door. As the bell above the door rang, the man walked up the steps to become a giant once again. The boys peeked back in the window and saw the Giant waving back at them.

"Get your filthy hands off of my window, ya little buggers", the man said under his breath, smiling through clenched teeth as he waved goodbye.

  As the boys walked along, Art couldn't stop talking about what they'd just seen. "He was huge! And did you hear how he talked? He ain't from around here. He wasn't Italian. He sounded like he was from England or London, one of those countries…"

  Phil just walked along, amazed that he had been face to face with a Giant.

THE ATTIC

  Art ran through the kitchen shouting, "Mom! MOTHER!" Racing into the living room, Art was bursting with excitement. "I saw a real life Giant!

97

MOM! Where are you?"

"I'm up here, but you wait right there. I'll be right down."

Art and Phil continued up the stairs and got to the top just as the surprised mother pushed a box up into the attic. Hearing the kids, she quickly stepped down off of the ladder, "I told you to wait downstairs, didn't I? Now go back downstairs, I'll be there in a minute."

"But we saw a giant. A GIANT! He was ten feet tall and eats a pizza the size of this house!"

Art's mom seemed taken off guard and quickly put the steps to the attic away. "What are you talking about, a giant. There's no such thing as a giant, not since David slew Goliath." She corralled the boys back down the stairs and told them to settle down. "You've had too much caffeine; I can tell by the way you're ranting. No more soda's for you."

"But, mom…! He's down at Big Tony's. You've got to go see him." Art was on the verge of screaming. "I don't have to go anywhere. You boys just go play in the basement until Phil has to go home. It's almost time for the streetlights to come on." Her stern voice meant business.

"Alright... but we did see a giant...," Art said, defeated.

"I'm sure you did, Arthur. I'm sure you did."

The boys bounded down the basement stairs and started bouncing a basketball on the cement floor. Phil dribbled the ball and asked Art, "What was your mom hiding in the attic?" Art stole the ball from him and asked what he meant.

"At my house, if my mom puts anything in the attic it's because she's hiding it from us. Christmas presents, birthday presents, old pictures of her smoking cigarettes... You know, stuff she doesn't want us kids to see." Phil's voice went into a whisper, "I wonder what your mom's hiding from you? " With that, he stole the ball back from Art and started dribbling again.

"She *did* put the ladder up right away, didn't she?" Art thought aloud.

"Yep. And I'll bet you a dollar that there's something in that attic that you aren't supposed to see." Phil handed the ball over to Art, "I've got to go home. If I'm late for supper one more time this week I'll get grounded. Halloween's almost here and I can't mess up. If I do my mom won't let me stay out late and Trick or Treat. See ya, wouldn't want to be ya."

  "Yeah, see you tomorrow...," Art dropped the ball and headed up the stairs, wondering what was in that mysterious box.

GETTING INTO THE SPIRIT

  Art was the first kid out of his seat when the school bell rang. He raced to his locker, threw some books inside and grabbed his backpack. Just as he slammed the locker door he heard the voice that he was hurrying so quickly to avoid. "Hey Art! I hear you saw a Giant! Did you see the bearded lady too?" Bauer the bully stood between Art and the exit. "Hey Art, you know what?" Bauer suddenly quizzed. "What...," Art said, trying to get to the door. "That's what!" Bauer knocked the backpack out of Art's hands, sending it crashing to the floor. Bauer then walked away, laughing. It was moments like this that Art wished Phil went to his school. At least Phil could have warned him when the bully was sneaking up on him. Every day there was a showdown at the locker, and Art was the one that was always humiliated. It wouldn't have been so bad if Becky

Peppler's locker wasn't three down from Art's. And Becky Peppler, Art thought, was beautiful.

Art picked up his stuff and put his head down and ran for the door. Once outside, some of the kids were talking about Halloween. "I'm going to be a vampire." "I'm going to be Spiderman." One of the kids shouted to Art, "What are you going to be for Halloween, Art? Are you going to be a Giant?" The kids all laughed at Art as he continued walking.

Once home, he quickly performed his chore of feeding the cats, and shouted to his mom that he was going down to Phil's.
"Okay, but be home in an hour so you can get your homework done before supper. We're having Hungarian Goulash to get us in the mood for Halloween. Get it? *Ghoul*-lash? Oh, I slay me..."
"Alright...," Art shouted as he disappeared out the back door.

Phil was waiting at the alley. "You want to go look in the window at the pizza shop and see the Giant? My mom said I could."

Art looked disappointed, "I don't have any money..."
"I didn't say we'd buy anything, just go peek in the
window and run." Phil made it sound so safe.
"What if he catches us?" Art asked, concerned.
"We'll just peek in and run, he won't even see us.
C'mon." Phil led the way.

As they walked, Art kept an eye out for his dad. He
hadn't asked permission to go off of the block, so he
didn't want to be seen. "Let's go all the way down
the alley and cut over, you want to?"
"...past Lohsie's Woods?" Phil asked in disbelief.

"Yeah, it's daylight so it won't be so creepy. We'll be
okay. Besides my dad will be coming down the street
on his way home from work. If he sees me I'll be
grounded for sure. Let's take the alley...," Art said,
struggling to keep up with Phil.

As they rounded the corner at the pizza shop, they
crept up to the window and smashed their faces
against the window. They could see the Giant
throwing pizza dough high into the air. No one was
in the shop so the boys stood and stared for a
moment. Then suddenly, The Giant looked out the
window and saw them, their hands and faces pressed
up against the once clean window.

Both boys yelped and pushed away from the glass, tumbling over each other as they made their escape. Inside the shop, the pizza dough dropped through the man's hands, landing on the floor. "Bloody lads...! First they smudge my window and now this!" He angrily picked up the dough and tossed it into the trash. Racing down the steps, he lifted the door on the counter and ran to the front door. "You kids stop touching my window! You're smudging it with your filthy fingers!"

The boys didn't stop running until they had crossed the street and were safely on their own block. "That was a close one...," Art panted as he buckled over to catch his breath.

"Too close...," Phil agreed. "Did you hear him yell at us? He chased us out!"

"I know, but I didn't look back!" Art laughed.

"Me either! That was awesome. You know what I'm thinking?" Phil said with a grin. Art looked up at him but said nothing.

Phil went on, "I'm thinking that this year's Hallow's Eve is going to be the best ever! We ought to spray

shaving cream on his windows!"
Art looked shocked, "No way!"

Phil was determined, "We'll write something' in shaving cream and make prank calls to Big Tony's! We'll ask for the Jolly Green Giant! It'll be funny!" "It won't be if we get caught! You're crazy..." It was obvious that Art didn't want to have anything to do with it.

"Art, Halloween is in four days! Who better to mess with than the Giant?" Phil was beside himself with excitement. "...Aw, man, this is going to be great!"

Art started walking away, "No way, Phil! I'm not going to get into trouble and have all my candy taken away."

Phil ran up in front of him and spun around, "We've got to get into the spirit of the holiday! Halloween is about the tricks, Art! My mom and dad said I can go out without them, as long as there's an adult in the group. Tell your mom and dad that you're going out trick or treating with me and my parents on Hallow's Eve and we'll go down to Big Tony's and mess with the Giant! They'll never find out!"

Art thought for a moment… "But what if we get caught? I won't be able to go out trick or treating, ever again, seriously. Besides, I don't want to lie to my mom…"

Phil realized that Art was chickening out.   "Well, maybe you're right. We should just go trick or treating with the little kids. Pulling pranks on Hallow's Eve is for the bigger kids anyway."
"Hey! I'm not a little kid." Art snapped back.

"I know you're not, that's why we should go crazy this year. Don't you know anything, Art? November 1st is All Saints Day. October 31st is Halloween! They used to call it Hallow's Eve because it was the night before the saints holiday. We can do what my brother and his friends do. We'll go out and pull pranks the night before anyone's expecting it! Get into the spirit of Halloween, Art. We don't even have to wait 'til Halloween night to have fun. Just think about it, will you?"

"Whatever…," Art mumbled. The boys parted ways when they got to Phil's yard. Art shouted, "I'll see you tomorrow. I've got to go eat supper. My mom's making Hungarian Goulash…"   "Did she make that goofy joke again?" Phil asked.

"Yeah, every year, she's in the Halloween spirit...,"
Art said walking away.

A CLOSE CALL

Art finished matching the list of words with the list
of definitions. English and Spelling came easy to him
so he didn't mind doing the homework. But the
Math sheet was different. He put it off until last,
hoping that some miracle would happen so that he
wouldn't have to face it at all.

Art's mom frantically searched through the
cupboard. "Oh, fiddlesticks! I have to go back to the
grocery. Shame on me for trying to remember
everything, I should have made a list! Arthur, your
dad will be home any minute now. You stay here and
finish your homework and I'll be back in a jiffy. Don't
leave that table until your homework's all finished.
I'll be right back..."   Kissing him on the forehead as
she rushed out, "Don't open the door for anyone,
you hear?" "I hear," Art shouted without looking up.

Art listened for the car door to slam and then
rushed over to the window. He watched the car
disappear down the street. Art quickly grabbed his

Math sheet and headed up the stairs to his room. Passing the entrance to the attic, he paused, looking up at the ominous plank of wood that covered the entrance.

Phil's words rang in Art's head over and over again. After hiding the Math sheet, Art went back into the hall. Reaching up, he grabbed the rope that hung down from the ceiling. Pulling hard, Art stepped back as the plank swung down, causing the ladder to unfold in two jarring movements.

Art looked up the ladder and could see the eerie darkness of the attic. Carefully, he climbed the ladder to the top. As his eyes adjusted to the darkness, he could see the box that his mother was hiding. What was in it? Was it for him? It sat in the darkness, alone and mysterious.

His concentration was shattered when he heard the distant slam of a car door. Crawling over to a window, Art could see his father getting home from work. Scrambling down the ladder, Art turned and quickly flung it upward, then slammed the door shut. Art raced down the steps and into the bathroom as the front door swung open. When he heard his dad enter the kitchen, Art came out of the bathroom trying desperately to "act normal".

"Oh, hi Dad, Mom went to the store and I'm already done with my homework," Art lied nervously.

The tired man went in and sat in his easy chair. He disappeared behind the newspaper just as Art crept by. Art made it down the three steps to the back door when he heard his father's voice, "Where do you think you're going, boy?"

Art looked up the stairs and there stood his father, towering over him with no hint of a smile on his face. Thinking fast, Art blurted, "... out?"
His father looked surprised, "But it's almost time for supper!" Then the tired man shook his head and said something that would stick with young Art for the rest of his life, "When will you learn? I'm not a king, and you're not a prince, so quit acting like one!"

Art stood at the door for a moment, stunned. Preferring not to cross paths with the angry adult again, he quietly slipped out the back door.

WHO'D A THUNK IT!

The next day the teachers and students were all talking about Halloween. Miss Brown made the kids read a story aloud about a guy that had a pumpkin head and rode a horse. That's all that Art got out of it because his thoughts kept drifting to the box in the attic.

As the kids took turns reading, the others sat nervously, trying not to attract the teacher's attention. If Miss Brown made eye contact with a kid that wasn't reading along like they should have been, she'd call on them to read next… and that meant getting up in front of the class. Art tried to be invisible because he had a slight lisp that always made the other kids giggle.

Thinking about the box, Art tried to picture what was in it. It wasn't his birthday and Christmas was still a month away so he doubted that it was a gift for him. But what could it be? And why was his mom being so sneaky about it? Art could hardly wait for the bell to ring so he could race home to find out.

Art heard the ruler smack down on the desk next to him. "Mr. Harter... Donald... DONALD!"

Sitting next to Art was the deaf kid who always brought candy into class. He couldn't hear the cellophane crackle when he opened each piece of candy. The other kids always giggled when they heard it because they knew that Miss Brown was going to have to take the candy away from him. Donald was always surprised when she appeared in front of his desk, ruler in hand, to take the treats away. But today Donald got lucky because the bell rang, setting off a stampede for the door.

"You got lucky this time, Donald...," her voice trailed off as she realized that Donald couldn't hear her as he rushed for the door. "Tell him not to bring candy to class tomorrow or he's getting a detention!" It was too late. She had lost control of the class as they funneled their way out into the hallway.

Art saw Bauer waiting at his locker, so he ducked into the nearest classroom. Peeking back out he saw that Bauer was looking around, probably waiting to pick-on Art one last time before he headed home. Art decided to wait, out of sight, until Bauer gave up and left the building.

"What are you doing in here, Art?"

Art swung around and found himself face to face with Becky Peppler. "Are you hiding?"

Art's face went red with embarrassment, "No! No! I just walked into the wrong class…" Not knowing what to do, he quickly gathered himself, and choosing his words carefully, heard his own voice say, "Can I walk you to your locker?"

Becky looked embarrassed as she turned slightly so that Art could see the other cheerleaders in the room. "Uh, no, we're having a pep meeting…"

Art's legs almost buckled out from under him. The other cheerleaders stopped talking amongst themselves long enough to stare and giggle. "Oh, sorry, um, I've got to go now, bye." He turned and bolted out of the door, stumbling right into Bauer the bully.

"Oh, there you are! I thought you were trying to avoid me or somethin'." Looking into the classroom and then back at Art, Bauer sneered. "What are you doin' with the pep squad, Art, teachin' them cheers?" The guys that were standing with Bauer started laughing and making fun of Art.

Just when he thought he was going to breakdown and cry, Art heard Becky's voice behind him say, "He's waiting for me. Quit being such a loser, Bauer." Art felt her slip her hand into his as she said, "C'mon, Arthur, walk me to my locker…"

The crowd of bully's parted, allowing Art and the beautiful Becky Peppler to pass through. Art couldn't feel his feet move as they floated dreamily down the hall. When they got to the lockers Art finally was able to speak. "Thanks, Becky. I thought you were having a cheerleading meeting…"

"We are. I just can't stand that stupid bully. I don't think it's right how he picks on you…" Becky blinked her big brown eyes.

Art couldn't believe this was happening. He was still holding Becky's hand! In disbelief, Art just had to ask, "Does that mean that you like me?"

Becky dropped her hand away from his and smacked him on the arm, "Shut up! I've got to get back to the meeting. I just couldn't stand to see you treated like that. I think you're…"

Suddenly a girl's voice bellowed, "BECKY! HURRY UP, WE'RE DECIDING ON THE DECORATIONS FOR THE PEP RALLY. WE'VE GOT TO VOTE! C'MON!"

Becky blurted, "I've got to go," and ran down the hall, her pony tail bouncing with each step.

Art shouted after her, "YOU THINK I'M WHAT?" Becky disappeared into the classroom, leaving a happy, but confused, Art standing alone in the hallway.

THE WORST IDEA EVER

That night Art was doing his homework at the kitchen table when his mom breezed through carrying laundry. She quickly took a step back and questioned the busy student. "Are feeling alright?" "Yeah, why," Art asked without looking away from his worksheet.

"I didn't have to tell you to sit down and do your homework. Did you feed the cats?"

Art responded, "Yepper doodle..." He had heard the expression from his grandpa and always thought it was cool.

His mother laughed, "Well, you are definitely up to something. You're either up to something or you met a girl. One or the other..."

Art looked up but she was already gone. "How does she do that...," he mumbled. The truth was that Art was guilty of both.

After dinner Art excused himself and went up to his room. He sat on his bed and thought about writing Becky a note. He actually wrote a couple of sentences but quickly tore it up so that no one would know what he'd written. He then opened his notebook to the last page and wrote *Art + Becky,* realizing how corny it was, Art slammed the book shut. "I'm such a dork!"

Art could hear his mom and dad discussing plans for a Halloween party. Each year they had Phil's parents over on Halloween night. Phil's parents always declined to come over for Hallow's eve because they worried that the neighborhood kids would vandalize their yard while they were gone.

"I have an idea, honey," Art heard his mother say. "Why don't we invite the Bauer's to our party this year? We never have before and their son is a friend of Art and Phil's. Oh, I think that's a good idea..."

Upstairs Art ran to the air vent so that he could hear them better. Their voices carried right up the vent like a speaker system between the two floors. Art's heart dropped. How could such a wonderful day end so badly? He had never told his parents how mean Bauer was because he, once in a while, would put up with Bauer so that he could play with his cool stuff. Besides, Art's mom wanted him to be nice to everyone. She wouldn't understand how awful the Bauer boy could be. And now the Bauer's were going to ruin Halloween for Art and Phil. Art could barely breathe. This was suddenly going to be the worst Halloween ever.

A RED FLAG DAY

Art was running late when he got to his locker. He threw his backpack into it and quickly grabbed a pencil and notebook. He took a pack of gum and his Mathematics book off of the shelf and slammed the door shut. Sprinting down the hall, he slowed down only when he got to the classroom door. Quietly, he opened the door and tried to slip in unnoticed.

"Nice that you could join us today, Arthur. The class was just getting out their assignment sheets so, by all means, join us won't you?" Mr. Miller hated tardiness, especially when it distracted the other students. "Does everybody have their assignments out? If so, we'll get started..."

Art's heart sunk. He realized that the assignment sheet that he was supposed to be looking at was still on his dresser... at home.

"Since you were nice enough to join us today, Arthur, why don't you come up to the chalkboard and show us what you came up with for problem one," Mr. Miller said, leaning against his desk. "Quickly now, we have a lot of ground to cover today."

Art looked around at the other students hoping one of them would volunteer to go first, but they just smiled back at him. Fumbling with his notebook, he hoped the sheet would miraculously fall out of it, answers and all, but Mr. Miller's voice boomed out once again.

"Arthur, are you not listening?" Then in a gesture that was meant to further humiliate him, Mr. Miller looked at Donald Harter and asked him who was supposed to be going to the chalkboard. Donald pointed at Art.

The teacher went on, "Now Donald understands what I'm saying, why don't you? So unless you have a problem, get up here and show the class how you worked out problem one on your worksheet."

"I have a problem...," Art mumbled.

"Let me guess, Bauer tore up your worksheet again." Mr. Miller said, frustrated.

"Uh, no, I left it at home...," was Art's weak reply.

Mr. Miller stood up straight and pretended to clean out his ear, "Excuse me? I don't think I heard you right. You left your homework where?" The other kids started to giggle. Art knew that he was in big trouble.

"At home, I left it at home." Art was ready for a long lecture, but Mr. Miller made it short and simple. "F".

Art was both surprised and terrified. "F?"

"F", the teacher repeated without explanation. He just turned around and began erasing the previous day's problems off of the board, clearing a space for the first student of the day... one that actually did their assignment.

Art spent the next hour listening to Donald Harter open candy wrappers and wishing that the school bell would ring to end his misery.

Finally the class ended, but Mr. Miller told Art to stay for a "chat". Trudging up to the big desk, Art quietly offered, "I'm sorry." Mr. Miller laughed out loud, "You don't have to apologize to me, Arthur. "You need to apologize to yourself because you are the only one that you let down. Do you understand me? Arthur, you're a smart kid. I know that math isn't the most exciting subject for you. You've got to find a way to make it interesting, whether you take it as a challenge to conquer, or a problem to solve, whatever. You just need to buckle down and catch up with the others. You got an "F" today, but tomorrow you may get a better grade... maybe even an "A". Now, why didn't you bring your assignment today, really?"

Art thought for a moment, trying to come up with an answer that would convince Mr. Miller to give him a second chance. An awkward moment passed before Art admitted, "I forgot..."

The teacher tried to understand, "You forgot..." "Yes, sir, I just forgot."

Mr. Miller stood up and tried one last time to inspire the lost student, "I'll make a deal with you, Arthur. You're waving the 'red flag' today, but if you can get an "A" on the next assignment, and I know you can. I'll let you teach the class. I'll sit in the back and you can sit at my desk and teach the class. How does that sound? You can talk about anything that's interesting to you. It doesn't even have to be math. It will be your day to show the class who Arthur really is."

With that said, Mr. Miller walked toward the door. "Just remember this, Arthur. It's always easier to 'keep up' than it is to 'catch up'."

ART'S CRY FOR HELP

All day long Art tried to concentrate on his school work. He knew that Mr. Miller was right about keeping up with his assignments. No one had ever explained it that way. Art felt like he could get a handle on his assignments if he kept up with each day's work. A simple concept but one that Art obviously hadn't been practicing.

At the end of the day he noticed that things were starting to look up. Bauer wasn't at his locker to pick on him, for one. And second, Becky was at her locker when Art walked up. "Hey Becky…"

Becky looked up and mumbled, "Oh, hi Art. Mr. Miller tore into you big time."

"Yeah…" Art said, embarrassed. "I goofed up, big time." Art closed his locker and started to walk away. Suddenly a thought struck him, turning around he took a couple of steps back toward Becky. "Hey, is there any chance that you could… I mean, you wouldn't want to…"

Becky laughed, "Spit it out, Art."

Art took a deep breath and tried not to lisp, "Could you help me with my math assignment? If you don't want to, it's okay…"

"Sure," Becky replied. "I've got cheerleading until four, but if you want, we can meet at the library when it's over, cool?"

Art asked, surprised, "Will the library be open?"

Becky laughed. "Yes, it will be open! The library is open until five every day. You really do need help don't you?"

Art blushed, "Yeah, but I want to start keeping up. You know, do better."

Becky smiled as she reached up to take lint off of Art's shirt, "You're cute... I'll see you at four!"

Art stepped aside to let her pass. As she walked off she put a baseball cap on and pulled her hair through the hole in the back. Art shouted, "Yeah, okay, see you at four!"

Becky met Art and helped him with his new math assignment. She was an "A" student, so it was easy for her to explain the process of solving the problems, but it wasn't always easy for Art to stay focused on the work. Each time Becky leaned against him his heart raced. When she looked into his eyes while explaining something, he held his breath.

But as he grasped the concept of problem solving he became more and more excited about the work. Soon he was working away at equations without

Becky's assistance. By the last problem, Art felt proud of the progress he'd made.

He was almost sad that the assignment was finished. Becky got up and put her hands on his shoulders and gave them a squeeze. "You got it figured out, Art! See! Just remember, don't avoid the problem. Face the problem, straight on. The key to math is taking it one step at a time."

Art smiled up at her and said, "Thanks, Becky, I really appreciate your help. And thanks for not laughing at me."

"No problem, *Arthur*!" They both laughed because everyone knew that he hated being called that. But out of her mouth it was music to his ears.

THE HALLOW'S EVE RAID

The night Art had dreaded finally came. He had heard that a lot of the bigger kids were going to throw toilet paper rolls into all of Mr. Lohsie's trees. It was an act that had become a Halloween tradition.

Art caved in and told Phil that he would go along with him on the shaving cream rampage. Phil had already hidden two cans of shaving cream behind the garage, so all they could do was wait for the sun to go down.

Art's parents were in the living room watching television. Upstairs, Art and Phil were looking up at the attic door. "I'll bet it's a dead rabbit... or a human heart!" Phil suggested. "That box is just the right size for a human heart."
Art thought for a moment, "Why would my mom have a human heart in a box?"
"I don't know. It's almost Hallow's Eve... anything's possible."

A booming voice came echoing up the stairs, "You boys are a little too quiet up there. If you're thinking about going into that attic, you can forget that idea right now."

Art's eyes bulged out in disbelief. "How does she do that!"

The boys went out into the garage and just messed around. They put air in Art's bike tires and tore the tape off of the handle bars to make it look "cool". It started to get dark so the boys had to turn the light on in the garage. "Now's the time...," Phil said as he looked out the window. "It's time for Operation Shaving Cream".

Art had second thoughts as they walked, shave cans in hand, down the alley toward Big Tony's Pizza. "Are you sure this stuff won't mess up the window, you know, permanently."

"Naw, don't worry, this is going to be awesome." With the confidence of a soldier, Phil marched a few feet ahead of Art.

"The Giant isn't going to like this," Art said, jogging to catch up.
Phil looked back, smiling, "I know! He's gonna roar!"

From a distance they could see The Giant making pizza's in the window of the shop. The boys ran around to the side of the building to plan their attack.

"I'm going to write 'Greenie Giant'. You know, like a giant booger. What are you going to write?" Art asked Phil.

"I don't know yet. One, two, three, let's go!" Phil jumped out of his hiding spot and ran along the building to the front. Art straggled closely behind.

They rounded the corner and, each shaking a can of shaving - cream, went into action.

Art waited for Phil to start spraying and then did the same. A big G, then a big R, the foam was going on as planned. Between letters Art glanced inside the window at the counter. The customers and The Giant were looking at a menu.

"Hurry up! I'm almost done!" Phil ordered.

Art resumed spraying and quickly finished his part. Dashing away, giggling with every step, they couldn't believe that they actually did it. Once they were safely on their block the boys high-fived each other and threw the empty cans into a trash can.

"Man, The Giant is going to be mad!" Phil smiled and looked at Art. "We really showed that giant! Let's go back and check it out from across the street. You want to?"

Returning to the scene of the crime, the two vandals crossed the street at the far corner, then went from bush to bush until they got a good view of their masterpiece. There on the big window written in shaving cream was GREN GANT and ART WAS HERE!

"GREN GANT? Who is Gren Gant?" Phil looked at Art
with squinted eyes. "You panicked!"

Art looked at his botched job and shouted, "Aw
man, I spelled it wrong!" Suddenly realizing what Phil
had written, Art exploded, "WHY DID YOU PUT *MY*
NAME?"
Phil laughed hysterically, "Duh! I wasn't going to
leave *MY* name!"

On their way home they could see Lohsie's newly decorated tree in the front yard. The toilet paper blew with the breeze as it hung down off of nearly every branch. Phil's older brother, Brad, had just thrown the last roll into the tree. Phil watched him dash off to catch up with the rest of his friends.

The boys split up and headed for home. Hallow's Eve had been a total blast.

HALLOWEEN DAY

The school janitor was busy pulling toilet paper out of a tree when the students began to arrive. Buses dropped off screaming kids, too excited to stay quiet on this very special day. Not only was it a Friday, but it was also Halloween.

Art slipped a note into the crack of Becky's locker. As the paper dropped in he had second thoughts, but it was too late. The note was now securely inside. Art only hoped that his thank you note didn't sound stupid or corny. He questioned whether he had spelled everything correctly, and wondered if she would still think he was "cute" after reading it. Anyway, he had to let her know once again that he appreciated the help with the Math assignment. And deep down, he didn't want the communication between them to end.

Bauer walked up to his locker but, strangely, didn't acknowledge Art. Art stood there, helplessly waiting for harassment... but nothing. Bauer did the combination to his lock and opened the door. Without looking up he said, just loud enough for Art to hear, "My mom's making me go over to your house tonight. Are you dressing up to go Trick or Treating'?"

"Yeah, I guess." Art said, acting uninterested. Bauer slammed his locker door and turned to walk away.

"Are you?" Art asked.

The bully looked back, "Yeah, right!"

Art moved slowly toward his Math class, scanning his completed assignment sheet as he walked. Mr. Miller was already at his desk, asking the students to bring their assignment up to him. "Put it right here on this stack. We're going to do something a little different today. Being that it's Halloween, we'll spend our time today working on the problems on page 57 of your text. Now, that should make sense because you worked on page 56 yesterday…"

One of the students shouted, "We're doing our homework in class today?"

"That's right. I'm giving you a break this weekend, if you can finish your assignment while I'm grading yesterday's work, you won't have homework to do over Halloween weekend. And I won't spend my weekend grading papers. Sound good?"

The kids formed a line up to his desk and, one by one, dropped their assignment on the pile. As Art approached, Mr. Miller acted surprised and joked, "Well, well, Art. You're right on top of things today. Good for you…" Art smiled back at him nervously.

Art settled in at his desk and began the long process of solving the equations on page 57. It felt good working out each problem. Thanks to Becky, he understood what he was doing for the first time since the school year began. He had just needed a private tutor and the motivation to put him on the right path. The fact that he had a crush on her was motivation enough to do better. He didn't want to embarrass himself anymore. From now on he was determined to do the best that he could and hand his assignments in on time.

The hour long class seemed to last forever. Art tried to stay focused on the work. Once in a while Mr. Miller would ask him to get Donald Harter's attention. "Tell him to put that candy away and get back to his assignment, please. Thank you."

Finally, Mr. Miller stood up and asked everyone to put their pencils down for a moment. "I have an announcement. Listen up, everybody. Next Monday is a special day. I made a deal with one of my students and, being a man of my word, I'm going to honor that commitment. I won't be teaching the class on Monday. You're going to get a break from me, just for the day, so don't get too excited. It's just for one day... but Arthur will be up here and I will be back there. So, just hold onto your assignments and we'll get back to them on Tuesday." Suddenly, the school bell rang. The students looked at Art, wondering what was going on, as Art ran up to see Mr. Miller.

"No, way... I got an 'A', for real?"

" Well, actually, you got an 'A-', but that's good enough for me. Good job, Arthur, I knew you could do it." Mr. Miller looked pleased. "See, it helps if you do the work and then bring it to class. It's half the battle."

"Awesome! But what am I supposed to do on Monday?"

"Whatever you want... you've earned it."

After school, Art and Phil met at the alley behind Lohsie's woods. The tree's looked strange with toilet paper still hanging off of them. Phil looked over the damage in disbelief, "Those guys are so lucky that Lohsie didn't catch them. They'd be buried in those woods right now if he had."

Interrupting, Art shouted, "Aw, man, I forgot the big news! My mom invited the Bauer's over to the party tonight," Art announced this as though it was the end of the world. "...and we're the ones that have to deal with the bully!"

Phil tried to be optimistic, "Maybe he won't come with them..."

Art was already shaking his head, "No, he's coming."

Phil shook it off, "We'll just ignore him, that's all. If he acts like a jerk we'll just lose him and meet back at the garage."

"Yeah, I guess. But no matter what, we can't let him take charge of everything. He'll be on my turf and he isn't going to boss us around tonight. But I still wish he wasn't coming." Art changed the subject quickly, "I wish we could get into the attic to see what's in the box. It's driving me nuts. I almost wish I'd never seen mom putting it up there at all."

Just then, Art's mother's voice bellowed out across the neighborhood, "AR-THUR, TIME TO COME HO-OME!"

"Dang it! How does she do that! It's like she knows when I'm talking about her! G'yall! I'd better get home. I want to get my chores done 'because I know she's gonna want me to help her get ready for tonight." Punching Phil on the arm he continued, "You better get there early, dude. Don't leave me stuck hanging out with Bauer... I'll catch you later."

HAPPY HALLOWEEN!

So much for not letting Bauer boss them around. He showed up at Art's front door with his electric skateboard under his arm. The minute Art and Phil saw it they started begging, "Aw cool, can I ride it? Can I ride it?"

Bauer the bully knew how to handle them. Either threaten them to get what he wanted, or flaunt the cool toys that he had. Luckily, tonight he was willing to share. All three boys ran out to the driveway and took turns riding the contraption. Bauer rode it first, for what seemed like an hour, before finally handing it over to Art. After explaining how the handheld controller worked he stepped out of Art's way.

Phil and Art had seen Bauer riding it before but never had the chance to ride it themselves. Art's Batman cape kept getting caught in the wheels so Phil grabbed the controller from him. "You can't even ride it right. I'll show you..." Phil zoomed off and then crashed hard into the garage.

"Alright, that's enough for you guys. It's my turn!" Bauer checked the board for damage and then jumped on and rode out into the street and down the block.

"Well, that was fun." Art watched Bauer disappear down the street.

"Maybe he won't come back...," Phil said hopefully.

A group of kids came up the street carrying plastic pumpkins and plastic bags. Their costumes ranged from store bought super hero costumes down to the sheet over the head "I'm a ghost" variety.

Art and Phil were just getting to the age where they thought Trick or Treating wasn't cool, but still weren't crazy enough to pass up the chance to get loads of candy for free. So they made fun of everybody's costume as they joined the crowd, but quickly got swept up in the fun of Halloween.

Art's mom shouted orders to him, embarrassing him in front of the group. So he shouted back, "I WILL, G'YALL!" Then looking through his mask at the other kids said, "Moms are so dumb..."

In the distance Art's mom's shouted, "I HEARD THAT!"

Art looked over at Phil in his Superman get-up. Even through his disguise Phil knew what Art was thinking. "You're mom's psychic, dude."

The kids went to all of the houses that had porch lights on. When they got to Old Man Lohsie's, they dared each other to go up and knock on the door. Bauer rode up on his skateboard and shouted, "Go up there! Chicken... bawk, bawk, bawk chicken!"

"Why don't you go up, Bauer? If you're so brave..." The kids tried to taunt him into it, but he just rode on past.

"Why don't you have a costume, Bauer?" Phil shouted.

Looking back, Bauer shouted, "Because I'm not a chump like you guys are!"

Undaunted, the group moved past Old Man Lohsie's and went on to the next house. Before they knew it, they had covered their whole block and were on the next street over. Batman and Superman slowed down as the gang walked up to the pizza shop.

"We can't go in there, Phil." Art said, genuinely concerned.

"Aw, c'mon, you're in a costume! He won't see you, Art, he'll see Batman! He won't even know who we are." Phil hoped what he was saying was right. "He already washed it off the windows so he's probably forgotten all about it by now."

"I hope so...," Art said quietly as they followed the group of vampires, ghosts and football players.

Stepping inside the shop, they could see the Giant where he always stood. One of the kids shouted "Trick or Treat!" The Giant turned around with a smile, showing the unprepared kids a pair of vampire fangs!

The kids stopped cold for a moment, not knowing how to react to this adult holding a knife and wearing fangs. "I got you, didn't I chaps! Don't worry, I was just havin' you on. Halloween's not just for kids now, is it? No, no..." Walking down toward the register as he pulled the plastic fangs out of his mouth, he took the two steps down to floor level.

Art and Phil were dumbfounded. They saw that The Giant wasn't a giant at all. Art ran to the counter and stood on his toes to see over the counter. He could see the steps leading up to the platform where the pizzas were made.

"Take a handful but don't be too greedy. There's going to be a lot of other monsters coming in tonight. Got to save a bit for all of them, right?"

Art and Phil stayed close behind the others and reached their hands out to get their share. They didn't want to get too close just in case he recognized them from the night before. Quickly and as a group, the kids yelled, "Thank you!" and headed out the door.

Waiting outside was Bauer. "Hey, Art! You're mom said that she ordered a pizza and all you have to do is pick it up. Handing Art some money he added, "And she wants the change back."
Art looked at Phil, "What do we do?" Phil thought for a moment and said, "Get the pizza! He won't recognize us in our costumes."

Art suddenly remembered, "Oh yeah, duh, but you go in with me."

Batman and Superman went back into the shop, unafraid. The pizza man turned around, fangs and all, and smiled. "Oh! You're back! Weren't you just with that last lot?"

Batman stepped forward, "Yes, sir. My mom said I have to pick up a pizza…"

The pizza man smiled bigger than ever, "Oh, right. I've been waiting for you. I've got it right here. I've taped it shut in case you drop it or something. It's on the house, you just get it to your mum right away, you don't want it to get cold now, do you lad?"
"Thank you…"
"And boys, Happy Halloween!"

Batman and Superman scampered out of the door, sounding the bell as they left.

"That's cool, we're having' pizza tonight!" Art adjusted his mask so that he could see where he was going. "I can't believe he's not a real giant."
Phil agreed, "I know, pretty weird, huh?"
Art remained silent.
"Seriously, Art, it was cool thinking that he was!"
"Yeah, I guess you're right. So what if he's not a real giant. The Loch Ness Monster's still real, right?"
Phil bolstered his friend, "Heck yeah! Someday we're going to become scientists and go see 'Nessie', for real!"
Art felt better, "You're right, yeah! Oh, well, it doesn't matter. We're still having an awesome

Halloween, right?"

Phil shouted back at him, "That's right, we've got PIZZA!"

Bauer was waiting for them at Art's house. "Better get it in there, they're gettin' hungry!" Art and Phil took off their masks and went through the back door shouting, "PIZZA'S HERE!"

The adults looked up as they directed the boys to come to the table. They cleared a spot for the box and took a knife and began cutting through the taped edges. "Why don't you boys take the first slice...?" Art's mom said as she held up a camera and pointed it at the boys.

Phil, Bauer and Art said, "SURE!" Together, they opened the box. "WHAT THE...! Their mouths flew open in surprise as the flash of the camera caught their reaction. There, inside the pizza box, was a neatly formed mound of shave foam!

Art and Phil looked at each other, sure that they were in big trouble.

"Are you surprised?" Art's mom stood proudly. "The pizza man was surprised last night and just wanted you boys to know that he's got his eye on you."

Art mumbled, "Big Tony?"

"Yes, the man that owns the pizza shop. Shame on you kids for pulling a stunt like that. Now you kids are going to go back there tomorrow and apologize to him."

"Yes, mam," the boys said in unison as they walked away from the table.

"Now wait, we haven't excused you yet." Art's dad said firmly. He didn't speak often, but when he did, Art listened.

Art's mom went on, "To show you that we're kids at heart, we want you to have this." She turned and opened the door to the broom closet and returned with a box... the same box that the boys had seen her hiding in the attic.

The boys jumped and squealed with excitement. Art looked at Phil and smiled from ear to ear. "Go ahead, open it up!" Art's dad said from across the table. Art's mom quickly wound the camera, preparing to take the next picture. "All three of you boys get in there, now open your gift..."

Excited, Art took the top off of the mysterious box. POP! Something exploded out of the box, flying high into the air and sending the boys tumbling backwards. The camera flashed as the boys let out screams. The adults were still laughing as the boys cautiously stepped back up to the table. Phil picked up the Jack-in-the-Box as if it was from outer space.

"Happy Halloween, boys, we just wanted to give you a scare while you're still young enough to fall for it!" Art's mom tried to hug him but he pushed her away, still embarrassed that he had screamed so loud. "I wasn't scared…"

Art's dad laughed, "Of course not, boy, of course not." Looking at the other parents he said, "You can spend thousands of dollars nowadays to entertain these kids, but you still can't beat a good ol' Jack-in-the-Box to entertain the parents!"

The boys turned and headed back outside after sharing a laugh with the old folks. It turned out to be a Halloween that they would cherish for the rest of their lives.

THE MONDAY AFTER

Art took his place at Mr. Miller's desk and waited for the students to settle down. Clearing his throat and fumbling with the loose pages he held in his shaking hands, Art took a deep breath and began to read... "I knew I'd be a little nervous so I wrote everything down. Today instead of doing Math, I'd like to read you this story, it's called Hallow's Eve - The Best Halloween Ever..."

Looking across the room he could see Becky listening intently. She smiled at him, giving him the courage to continue on...

"Once upon a time there was a ten foot tall Giant..."

HIGH SCHOOL DAZE

Life for the kids around Lohsie's Woods began to change in ways they never imagined. As they entered high school, many of the kids drifted apart. Many of the things that were fun to them before suddenly became "uncool". Playing street football was replaced by going to the local McDonalds, a favorite meeting place of the high school crowd. The streetlights no longer dictated when they had to come home. Stories about Old Man Lohsie no longer struck fear in their hearts.

 Lohsie's Woods was still an eerie place. But the old man was seen less frequently until finally, no one could recall the last time that he was seen at all. His old junker sat in the woods until, eventually, nature took it over. It sat eerily alone in the woods, seemingly waiting for the old man to come out of the house. But the screen door would never slam shut again, signaling the kids in the area that "Lohsie's coming!"

PART FOUR - BEAR LAKE CAMP

The van slowed to a crawl as it ambled down the narrowing path. Through the pines, the lake shimmered under the bright summer sun. The volunteers, mostly students from South Side High School, had agreed to help out as counselors for the weeklong summer camp. Some signed on for the extra credit it provided toward graduation. Others just wanted to get away from home, thinking that it would be a carefree vacation. Art, now a soon-to-be senior, was there for a different reason... to meet girls. A lot had changed since the days of choosing hide and seek over girls. Just playing around Lohsie's Woods was "kid stuff" now. Art needed to spread his wings.

As the van pulled up to an opening in the woods, the kids suddenly grew silent. There in front of a wood-frame cabin sat a row of wheelchairs. Art finally broke the silence, "Hey, what are all of the wheelchairs for?" The others kids laughed, thinking that he was joking. The girl sitting next to Art asked, "Are you serious?" The driver shut off the engine and announced to his passengers, "They're for the campers. Welcome to Bear Lake, your home for the next week. This is a camp for kids that are just like you; the only difference is that these kids have Muscular Dystrophy. Everybody out of the van and we'll huddle up at the picnic tables for a quick orientation."

Art knew what kind of camp they had signed up for, it just hadn't sunk into his thick skull that some of them would require wheelchairs. He really knew nothing about the disease but jumped at the chance to go and perform magic, do some juggling, and generally entertain the young campers. But seeing the row of empty wheelchairs reminded him that these kids were fighting the battle of their lives. As he stepped out of the van he looked at the driver, "You mean these kids are-"

"...Rollers? Yep. Some of them have been in chairs their whole lives..." the driver interrupted. "Every one of these kids has looked forward to this day for the last year. It's our job to make sure that they have the best summer of their lives. Can you think of a better way to spend the next week?"

"No, I guess not..." Art mumbled.

"Alright, the kids are due to start arriving in about an hour so start unloading your stuff and put it right over here. We'll get our cabin assignments and find out who we will be paired with as soon as I find the lady in charge, O.K.? And, oh yeah, I've got to visit the bathroom. If anyone else needs to go they are right over there." Before the words were out of his mouth, a throng of kids dashed past him, racing toward the little building. The man let out a sigh, "Great... I can tell already, this is going to be a long week."

The camp director stepped out of the cabin letting the screen door slam behind her. The volunteers snapped to attention at what, at first impression, sounded like a gunshot. One of the volunteers clutched his chest and feigned a heart attack. As the startled kids broke into laughter the director made her way down the steps, "Sorry 'bout that! I always forget that door does that! It doesn't even faze me anymore." Joining the group she introduced herself, "Welcome to Bear Lake Camp, everybody. I'm Joan. I'm the camp director here and want to thank each of you for joining us this year. The work you do here, well, I don't know if 'work' is the right word, is going to make the difference between us providing just a regular old camp experience for these special kids, or us providing a camp experience that is nothing short of spectacular. And I'll tell you right now, people, you are going to reap the rewards of your efforts when you see a kid's face light up with joy. It's worth all the money in the world, I'll tell you. Oh, by the way, you do know you aren't getting paid for this, don't you?'

  The teenagers all laughed and made comments as though they thought otherwise.

  "You knew that! Anyway, your heart will be paid ten-fold by the end of the week..."

  Art looked over at the girl next to him and smiled. She smiled back but quickly turned her attention to the director.

  We've got about a half an hour before the kids start arriving so let's all walk over to the first-aid cabin to meet the camp nurse. She'll be giving you your assignments this year. We've found that it's best if she does the assigning of campers because she can fill you in on any special needs that an individual

147

might have." With that the director turned toward the row of chairs.

Turning back abruptly, Joan announced, "Oh, and no one is to sit in or play around with these wheelchairs. They are extras for the campers in case some of the 'walkers' need a break or get tired. We just want them on the ready at all times... moving on!"

Art walked up next to her and introduced himself. Joan interrupted quickly, saying "I know who you are! Thank you for coming to help out. We may not pair you up with anyone so that you can be free to help us with all of the crafts and entertainment stuff. Does that sound alright to you?"

Surprised, Art fumbled, "Well, yeah, whatever." Inside, he felt relieved. All of the special needs talk was kind of scaring him.

Joan spoke up, "I'm sorry, were you going to ask a question?"

Art spoke shyly, "You said 'walkers', what did you mean?"

"Oh, 'walkers' are just what it sounds like. Some of these kids are in varying stages of Dystrophy. Most of them this year are in wheelchairs 24/7, but some, the 'walkers', haven't degenerated to that point. But we keep the chairs around, just in case."

Art said nothing as they approached the next cabin. His heart sunk as he thought about what awaited him when the campers got there. Seeing empty wheelchairs was one thing, but being face to face with the ailing kids might be too much for him to handle. The sadness of the situation was creeping in.

After meeting "Nurse Dawn", Art stepped back and watched the process at hand. Each teenager was called up and given a name of a camper, a brief medical report on that kid, and handed a urinal. The look on each counselor's face matched what Art was feeling inside. *A URINAL! You've got to be kidding...*

Art was so relieved that he was helping with entertainment. All he had to do was help with some crafts, probably drawing pictures and gluing macaroni onto paper, and keep them happy by making them laugh. That's a lot easier than what the other volunteers had to do. They were going to have to *work*.

The girl that had caught Art's eye came walking up wearing a frown. Not sure of how to start a conversation, Art asked, "Did you get a camper?"

"Yeah, his name is Denny Ferguson.

"Is he a 'walker'?" Art asked, proud to show off his knowledge. "No. He's in an electric wheelchair but needs help with a lot of things. At least I won't have to push him." The look on her face was of worry and dread. "Nurse Dawn said that he's really quiet. She said that last year he was so quiet that they thought he was autistic or somethin'. She said he only talked to his family. If he's still like that I'm in trouble. How am I supposed to entertain him?"

Art thought for a moment, "You won't have to. If the kids quiet, just talk out loud but don't expect him to answer. It doesn't mean he's not having fun. Think about it. If you were him wouldn't you just be glad to be here?"

She smiled, "I guess..."

Art continued, "Don't worry. I won't have a camper so I'll be able to help you out."

"ARE YOU SERIOUS? YOU'D DO THAT FOR ME!"

Art grinned, "Yes. But you've got to do something for me."

The cute girl slapped his arm, shouting, "Whatever!"

"You've got to tell me your name!"

"OH, DUH! I'm Denise, I live in Columbia City.

"That's why I've never met you. My name is Art."

Nurse Dawn shouted out over the crowd, "Time to head up the trail, the kids are arriving. We'll greet them and then I'll point out your cabins. Remember, these are the strongest kids you will ever meet in your lives. Look past the chairs. Look past the physical condition of some of the more extreme cases because, counselors, there are no disabilities here. This is their week to just be kids at summer camp. Let's show them a great time!"

As the crowd of teens headed down the trail, Art noticed that Denise was right by his side.

WILD BOYS

Several vans were lined up by the director's cabin. A humming sound could be heard as Art and Denise got nearer. On the side of the first van was a platform lift. An excited kid sat in his chair, shouting instructions to his mother as she operated the lift. "Hurry up. Hurry up! Doesn't this dumb thing go any faster? It's gonna take all day!"

Joan stood beside Art and Denise, "That's Michael Ferguson. He was here last year. He's the most outgoing of three brothers. Once he gets excited, it takes him hours to come down."

Once the platform touched the ground the mother unlocked the wheels of the chair and Michael immediately shot forward, causing his mother to shout, "Be careful!" Michael, with the touch of a finger, maneuvered himself into a circle. Going round and round he shouted, "OH NO! It's going crazy! I can't stop it!" Art jumped forward and tried to get a hold of the runaway chair. The boy's mother shouted, "CUT IT OUT, MICHAEL!"

Michael laughed and laughed as he rolled out of her reach. His mother looked at Art and apologized, "Don't mind him, he's a brat! He does that whenever we're out in public. I told him I'm going to quit taking him out if he doesn't stop it." Rolling up to Art and Denise, the crazy kid shouted, "SUCKER!"

Suddenly, a soft voice from inside of the van ordered, "MICHAEL! Quit goofin' around and help Dougie..." Michael turned and buzzed over to the platform. His little brother, Dougie, was situating himself for his ride down the lift. "Stop right there, Dougie. MOM! You've got to lock his wheels or he'll fall off..."

The boy's mother shouted back, "I know what I'm doing, now shut up and wait for your brother." Art was kind of shocked. This lady wasn't treating these kids with 'kid gloves' at all. In fact, she was yelling at them just like, well, like they were 'normal'.

"I don't know who your counselor's are but you better be good to 'em, because I may not come back to get you!" Turning back to the platform as it touched ground, her voice softened, "Okay, Dougie. We're almost there…" As she leaned over to unlock his brakes she gave him kiss on the head. Michael's voice boomed out, "Quit it, mom! Don't kiss him, it's gross!"

Once again, the soft voice bellowed out of the van, "Michael, SHUT UP!"

Art took it all in… this family was nuts. Stepping forward he tried to get a look inside the van. The boy's mother noticed, "Yeah, there's one more comin'. Last but not least, the boss of the world, Denny." Art shot a glance at Denise.

On to the platform rolled a gawky, black haired kid with glasses. Art's first thought was that this was the skinniest kid he'd ever seen. Almost skeletal, he sat upright in his chair like a ruler on his throne. It was easy to see that he really was the boss.

  The first thing that Art had noticed was how the younger brothers listened to his every word. When Denny said "Shut up!" The brothers would shut up. His head would tilt to one side and then the other as he guided his chair to the proper position on the ramp. When his mother tried to give him directions, he shouted, "I've got it, mom. Just wait a second." The mother turned to Art and exclaimed, "I pity the fool that has this one." Turning back she tried to kiss Denny on the forehead, "Aw, mom," he said in a whisper, go do that to Dougie, not me…"

  Nurse Dawn talked to Mrs. Ferguson for a moment then called Denise over. Art watched while she met her camper. From a distance it looked like Denny was ignoring her. *Well,* Art thought, *at least she was warned*.

INSTRUCTIONS FROM DIRECTOR JOAN

  Joan walked by and motioned to Art, "C'mon, take a walk with me up to the road. We need to make sure the 'Welcome Campers!' sign is still up. We prop it up at the entrance and it fell down last year. Some of the parents drove all the way down to Pretty Lake. This year I don't want a repeat of that." Her hiking pace was a little faster than Art's, leaving him a step or two behind. Turning slightly, Joan continued, "What I need you to do is go around to the cabins and introduce yourself to the kids. While you're there, go ahead and check on the counselors to see if they need anything."

Art struggled to keep up, "Okay. I can do that."

"We'll let everyone settle in until 11:30. At that time we'll lead everyone up to the flagpole. That's where we'll raise the camp flag. The attendant actually pulls the rope, but the kids get to feel like they are in the spotlight and raising the flag. It's all about the kids..."

THE BOYS TO THE RESCUE

Little Dougie rolled down the path at a snall's pace, his head jostling from side to side from the rough terrain. The birds overhead called back and forth to each other, sometimes flitting from tree to tree.

The humming of the chair startled the squirrels, causing them to stand erect before dashing off of the trail and into the woods.

Back at base camp, the new arrivals were being unloaded and met with old friends. The "newbies" were introduced quickly so they felt at ease. Parents milled around, not wanting to leave their babies, some for the first time ever.

Joan and Art walked back into the clearing and heard quite a ruckus. Michael Ferguson was zipping around shouting, "Dougie! Dougie! Where are you?" Denny rolled over shouting "Shut up Michael." "But Dougie's gone! He was here a minute ago." Denny spun his chair around to face him straight on, "You were watching' him. Where'd he go?" Panicked, Michael spun in a circle. "I DON'T KNOW!" Art ran over to him and got his attention. "Chill out, buddy. We'll find him. Where was he last?" Michael's face was red, "Chill out! Chill out! Are you crazy? Somebody stole my brother!" Denny shouted back, "NOBODY STOLE HIM, MICHAEL! Let's go look for him…"

As the pair rolled down the path toward the lake they realized that someone was following them. Without looking back, Denny shouted out, "Who's back there?"

Art simply said, "Me."

"Me, who" Denny returned.

"...Me, Art."

Denny shouted back, "You don't have to go with us. We're not babies."

Art was surprised, "I know you're not babies! You guys are cool, I'm hangin' with you. You got a problem with that?"

"Ouch, he told you Denny!"

"So it's like that, huh?" Denny's chair went into high gear, "You've gotta keep up if you want to hang with the big dogs!"

Michael laughed and barked like a dog, with Denny joining in. Art started barking too. Keeping up was not a problem but he stayed a short distance behind them. If they really thought they were fast he wasn't going to burst their bubble. "Slow down you guys."

There they were; the two brothers and Art, barking like dogs in the middle of the woods. Laughing like madmen, the "rollers" spun around and waited for the "walker". Looking past the two brothers, Art could see another kid coming back up the path, it was Dougie.

The boys met him and really let him have it. "WHERE DID YOU GO? DON'T DO THAT AGAIN, DOUGIE!"

Art was touched by the scene. It was obvious that these brothers were a team. As the boys headed back to camp, Dougie said nothing at all. Art walked up next to Michael and asked, "He's a shy one, huh?"
"Yeah, but he's just a little kid..."
A quiet voice disagreed, "I'm not little."
"You're littler than me, Dougie."
"So!"

Art asked Denny, "Do you guys always fight like this?"
Denny smiled and threw his head back, "Yeah, it's fun!"

Upon returning to the clearing Joan came over and warned the kids not to wander off without an aide. Michael spoke right up, "We had an aide, Art was with us."

Art smiled at Joan and glanced at the boys, "I think I'm going to have to hang with these 'big dogs' just to keep them out of trouble."

Michael laughed, "This is our camp, now! We're here to *cause* trouble! C'mon, let's go see if Jeff's here yet. C'mon, Art, come with us!"
"Who is Jeff?" Art asked, following.
"He's our cousin. We've got to find him 'cause he has the squirt guns..."

The camp was now buzzing with activity;   parents giving last minute instructions about medication, or "meds" as they were called, and counselors showing the new arrivals around. Art saw the other counselors struggling with their campers, trying desperately to relate to them without showing any signs of pity. They seemed to be talking down to them, treating them like delicate little babies that needed coddling.

The Ferguson boys were different. They didn't act like victims in need of caretakers, not at all. These boys took charge the moment their wheels touched the ground and left their van. They were a force to be reckoned with. Aside from the fact that they were all in wheelchairs, there was nothing about these kids that made them different than any other kid in the world.

Art glanced over at the Ferguson's van and saw Denise sitting with the luggage. "C'mon, Denise, we're looking for Jeff!" Art waved as he trailed the boys.
"Who's Jeff?" Denise shouted as she got up.

"He's the kid with the squirt guns!" Art announced, laughing, as Denise joined the Ferguson gang. She whispered a confession to Art, "I'm not sure what I'm supposed to be doing..."

"Right now your job is to keep up with these kids!" Art walked along and began filling her in on the day's agenda as the kids listened in.

"I'm not going to the flag raising stuff! It's stupid," Michael shouted angrily. They just pick a kid to pull the rope until it's all the way up the pole and then everybody goes crazy clapping. It's for the little kids. I've seen it a hundred times..."
"...a *hundred times*?" Art said, grinning at Denise.
"Yeah, I've seen it a hundred times." Michael started spinning his chair in circles just to annoy Art.

Looking at Denny, Art asked, "Has he seen it a hundred times, Hot Dog?"

Denny smiled at the sound of his new nickname but quickly glanced at Denise and turned away. Finding an opportunity to tease him Art spoke up, "Denny! Are you scared of girls?"

Michael moved forward to defend his brother, "He's not afraid of girls! He's not afraid of anything." A soft voice joined in, "He just doesn't know her yet, leave him alone." Denise looked over to see little Dougie. "I'm sorry Dougie, if you guys don't want a girl tagging along..."

Little Dougie said quietly, "It's up to Denny..." Art laughed, "C'mon, you guys, she's cool. We're not as cool as you, but maybe it'll rub off on us, right Denise?" Denise didn't know what to say, "Yeah, girls can be cool too."

The boys howled with laughter as they rolled down the path toward the flagpole. Denise stepped closer to Art, "Are they ever going to like me?"
Art whispered back, "Like you, yes. Admit it, never!"

UP WITH THE FLAG!

"Huddle up, campers. Huddle up! It's time to raise the Bear Lake Camp Flag! We need a volunteer to pull the rope... anyone? If I don't get a volunteer I'll have to pick someone."

Joan the director scanned the crowd of kids hoping that one would roll forward. Art shouted from the back, "I think Michael Ferguson wants to do it! Michael! Michael! Michael!" Denny and Dougie joined in while Michael turned to Art in disbelief. "Quit it! It's stupid!" Director Joan shouted, "Well, get him up here! C'mon, Michael, you're the man of the hour..."

Michael and Art made their way to the front of the crowd with Michael swearing revenge, "I'm gonna get you for this! I can't do it by myself, I can't pull the rope!"

"You can do it, and it's gonna be cool." Art quickly untied the rope from the flagpole and tied an end to the back of Michael's chair. Michael caught on immediately and started blabbering, "I'm gonna raise the flag, aren't I?

"You sure are, all by yourself." Art stepped back and looked at Director Joan. She was shaking her head and smiling, "You guys are nuts!" Looking to the crowd, she went on, "OKAY, CAMPERS! LET THE WEEK BEGIN!" With that she motioned for Michael and Art to raise the flag. Michael started rolling off away from the pole as the flag began to go up, up, up! Looking back, Michael shrieked with joy. The whole camp erupted in applause as the flag reached the top. Art ran and stopped Michael, slapping his hand in a high five.

 Shouts of "Way to go, Michael!" and "AWESOME!" brought a smile to his face. Art glanced at Denise and saw that she was leaning over, laughing and talking to Denny. Art realized that tears were welling up in his eyes, for the first time in his life he was so happy that he could cry.

 "I did it! I did it!" Michael shouted.
Art quickly gathered himself, "Yeah, you did. That was so cool! You rock, buddy! YOU ROCK!"

WAKE UP!

The sun rose over the sleepy little camp, each cabin eerily quiet in the early morning light. Only the sound of Director Joan's screen door pierced the silence, a brief clap loud enough to be heard, but distant enough to be ignored by the young campers and their aides.

Art peeked over the side of the bunk beds. Looking straight up at him was Denny Ferguson, his eyes big and brown with a glint of mischief, "You wanna go down to the lake?" Art rolled back on his cot and closed his eyes, "Let's sleep a little bit longer..."

Art lay motionless, his mind slowly drifting off toward slumber. A moment later it began, "Psst!" Art's eyes opened slightly.
"Psst! Art! You wanna go to the lake?" Seconds passed with no response from Art. Denny gave it another shot, this time singing melodically, "Art, let's go to the la-ace."

In the upper bunk Art's eyes opened wide as he broke into a grin. He sang back, "In a minute..." Suddenly, in a loud voice Denny shouted, "C'MON!

GET ME UP SO WE CAN GO TO THE FREAKIN' LAKE!"
On the other side of the cabin a faint voice warned,
"Denny! I'm tellin' mom you were cussin'."
"SHUT UP, DOUGIE! You're not tellin' mom anything.
WE'RE AT CAMP TO HAVE FUN, SO LET'S GO TO THE
LAKE AND HAVE FUN! I WANT TO GO FISHIN'!"

From outside of the cabin a voice could be heard,
"You-who? Is everybody decent?" Art knew right
away that it was Denise.

Denny shouted back, "No! Go away," and began
cackling. Art jumped down from the bunk and
scolded him. "Denny! Be nice..."
"I don't have to be nice! She's your girlfriend..."
"Denny, shush! She is not!" Art glared at the frail
boy. Turning his attention to the cabin door, Art
changed his tone, "The coast is clear, girl, c'mon in."

The boys immediately complained that a girl was
entering the cabin. "Get her outta here, I'm naked,"
Michael shouted as he squirmed to pull the sheet up
over his bare chest. "I don't have a shirt on!"

"Joan told me that I'll be Denny's aide as long as he
behaves." She shot a look at Denny but felt

uncomfortable seeing the boy laid out in his bed, stick thin and pale. Trying to appear calm, she went on, "She said that you were a handful and..."

"Oh, I am a handful..." Denny interrupted. Art quickly cut him off, fearing what might come next, "Denny! Cut it out! Denise is cool, she's here to help us and have fun too."

"She can't have fun with us, she's a girl. This is a boy's cabin. "She's not supposed to be in here." The look on Denise's face was of complete disappointment. She wanted to be accepted by the boys but didn't quite know how.

"That's not true; she's your aide and can be in here anytime she wants. In fact, if you're not nice to her we'll just have her stay in the cabin tonight. How would you like that... a girl in your cabin?" The boys joined in a chorus of arguments until little Dougie spoke up. "Will she take me to breakfast?"

The other boys grew quiet. Denise realized that the question was for her. "I'm sorry, what did you say, honey?" The fragile little boy looked up with his innocent eyes and mumbled, "Will you take me to breakfast? I'm hungry..."

A smile spread across the girl's face as she stepped closer, "Of course I will, honey. Let's get you up and go get something to eat. I'm hungry too." Art smiled, knowing that little Dougie had taken a liking to her. The truth was, so had Art.

JOAN'S DREAM CAR

The screen door was propped open to the cafeteria so the wheelchairs could roll right through. Nurse Dawn was scurrying around giving meds to those that required it, while Director Joan stood at the back of the room, periodically smiling and waving to kids as they arrived.

Most kids had little table tops that attached to their chairs, while others rolled right up to tables to eat. The boys made a bee-line for an empty table. Michael drove up and bumped it, backed up and bumped it again as he tried to situate himself. "Michael, cut it out! You're knocking the table," Denny shouted. "You guys, c'mon! Let's just have a nice breakfast with no fighting…"

"We're not fighting! He's just bumping the table. Michael, CUT IT OUT!" Art and Denise shared a glance... these kids were out of control! Art tried to take control of the situation, "You guys are going to have to behave..."

  With that, Denny snapped and said something that opened Art's eyes to what the week was all about. "We don't have to behave, we're at summer camp!" Art realized that the kid was right. As he scanned the room he saw a bunch of kids that, for this one week, had gotten out of their houses, out of their boring routines of being stuck at home and living as patients, to being regular kids away at summer camp. The wheelchairs and sickly appearance no longer mattered here. Here no one stared at them with looks of pity. There were other kids just like them, many of which they only saw at this time of year. They were just kids having fun.

  Art looked over at Denise, her deep brown eyes big with enthusiasm. She spoon fed little Dougie with a sweetness that touched Art's heart. Art was just a high school kid but he was beginning to understand the truly important things in life. His heart ached, not only was he realizing that he had a crush on Denise, but seeing these kids all together made him think that he could help make a difference in their lives.

Joan came over to the table and leaned down to have a word with Denise. Art couldn't quite hear what she was saying but hoped that it was nothing that would pull her away. Denise nodded and looked over at Art. Joan stood back up and told the boys how nice it was to see them back for yet another year. Denny got excited and asked her if she had gotten the new car that she had talked about the year before. "Why, yes I did, Denny. You've got a good memory." Denny smiled and rocked his head back and forth to straighten up in his chair. "I like cars. Someday I'm gonna get a Corvette."

Joan smiled, "Wow! That would be trouble, Denny. I've seen you drive your chair around here, you'd be a menace to the other people on the road!"

Denny laughed, "And the cops wouldn't be able to catch me. I'd drive a hundred miles an hour! Is your car here?"

Joan looked pleased, "Yes, it's out in the parking area. You can check it out, it has a big flower on the side. But don't bump into it! It hasn't even had its first scratch yet." She looked at Art and went on, "I have dreamed of getting this Volkswagen Beetle for years. It's just so cute..."

Art looked at Denny, "Well, Hot Dog, you want to go check it out?"

Excited, Denny shouted, "Heck, yeah!"

Denny was something else, Art thought. Here's a kid that was truly interested in cars, though he would never actually get to drive one. But still, he planned on getting a Corvette someday. Boys will be boys, Art thought. Maybe his dreams are what kept him going through his dismal reality. Or maybe he was unaware that life had dealt him a tragic hand. Or, maybe, just maybe, he refused to accept it.

"We'll be right back," Art said as he put a hand on Denise's shoulder. She looked up and smiled, "You boys and your cars! Dougie and I will be right here." Looking at Michael she asked, "Do you want to stay here with us or are you going to look at the car too?"

Michael, who was capable of feeding himself, said, "I'll stay..." Denise felt good that he chose not to go, it was a sign that he was beginning to let down his guard.

Denny raced ahead so that he could get to the car first. "Don't get too close, Hot Dog. Joan would freak if you put a big dent in the side." Art watched in fear as the boy rolled right up to the door before halting his chair. "It's okay, I'm a good driver. Hey, this is pretty cool." From his vantage point in the chair, he couldn't see inside so he started asking questions. "Does it have a stick shift? Is it a four speed? How fast does it go? Look at the speedometer; does it go to a hundred?"

Art grew tired of the questioning and told him to look for himself. "How am I gonna do that? I'm too short…" Denny looked frustrated, there was so much he wanted to see but it was just out of reach. Art said, "I'll pick you up…" Art leaned down and put the brakes on the chair so it wouldn't roll out from under him. Then carefully picked up the frail kid and held him up to the window. "Aw, cool! It's a four-speed and the speedometer goes to a hundred and she's got a peace sign hanging from the mirror and…" Art shifted the boy in his arms, his squirming around made it hard for Art to hold him.

Putting him back down in the chair, Art carefully stood up. "You're heavier than you look, Hot Dog."

"I know. I'm so skinny Mom calls me a bag of bones…" Art thought that was a little harsh. "Does it bother you?"

"No, because I know she's not lyin'. I used to weigh more, but I'm getting' skinnier now. Mom says she's gonna fatten me up, though." Art thought how difficult it must be to watch your child wither away. Most people would try to protect the kids to the point of lying, but it sounded like Denny's mom didn't pull any punches. "Your mom must be a tough cookie."

Denny nodded his head, "Yeah, she said God sent us to be a pain in her butt!"

Art had to laugh. These kids obviously were very close to their Mother. From what Art had seen, she would do anything for them without coddling them, and it made the kids stronger because of it.

Walking away Art turned and noticed that Denny wasn't coming with him. "Are you coming, Hot Dog? Let's get the others and go check out the lake, you want to?"

"Yeah, but aren't you forgetting somethin'? MY BRAKES ARE ON?!"

Art laughed and apologized, "Aw, dude, I completely forgot." Denny just shook his head, "You don't know much about cars, do you? You don't even know that you have to take the brake off..."

"Watch your mouth, boy. I'll forget to take them off now!"

"Okay, okay, I take it back. Let's go fishin'!" Art unlocked the brake and the two raced back to the cafeteria to get the rest of the gang. "I'm gonna make your girlfriend put the worms on my hook!"

 Art answered, acting irritated, "She's not my girlfriend! She's your girlfriend!"

 "Nuh-uh," Denny shouted…"She's Dougie's girlfriend!"

FISHING, SPITTING AND FALLING IN LOVE

 The morning was spent on the fishing pier. It was a sturdily constructed wooden structure that had railings on each side. The boys let Art and Denise bait their hooks and then took it from there. Casting out amounted to sticking the pole through the railings and letting the line drop.

 Michael especially enjoyed the outing, his love for fishing stemmed from watching hours of fishing shows on television. He spouted off information about fish and reels, things Art had never known. Denise stuck by Dougie, baiting his hooks, pulling on his line once in a while and suggesting that he "almost got one"! But all in all, the fishing was bad with no one was catching a thing.

"This is boring! I don't wanna fish anymore." Little Dougie said, disappointed. Michael agreed, "Hey, let's spit over the side. I'll bet the fish will come around then!" Before Art or Denise could suggest otherwise the boys were busy spitting over the railing. Laughing and spitting, they seemed to get more on themselves and the railing than in the water.
"You guys are gross...," Denise said, disgusted.
"That's because you can't spit like a boy can," Michael challenged.
Denise looked at Art, "I can spit further than Art can, and he's a boy!"

The boys went wild, "Dang, Art! You're not gonna let her say that, are you? She thinks she can spit better than you!"

Art saw that the kids were suddenly having fun again, "No way! Alright D, it's on!" He reeled back and let one fly. "There! Try beating that!" The boys were giggling as Denise stepped up to the railing. Art started chanting and the boys quickly joined in, "D, D, D, D...", until she let one fly.

"Aw, man! D beat you, Art! She beat you!" The laughter was a celebration.

"Well, I know when I've been beat. Good job, D! You win... *and* you have a new nickname!"

"D" looked into Art's eyes as she held up her hand for a high five. He smacked it, still lost in those eyes. She was so awesome to win those boys over the way she did. And those eyes! Art's stomach was a flutter with deep feelings he'd never felt before. This was no puppy love, this was real. For a brief moment Art forgot that the boys were even there. It was just him and the girl with the big brown eyes.
"Hey, you guys like each other!" Michael shouted. "Yeah, you two are lovers!" Denny joined in. "Art's got a girlfriend! Art's got a girlfriend! Art's got a girlfriend!"

Art and D, suddenly embarrassed, stepped apart and began wrestling with the boys. Everybody was having a great time on the pier at Bear Lake Camp.

TWO FRIENDS AND A BASKETBALL

Denny was the oldest brother and often felt that he was too big for many of the kid's activities that his younger brothers enjoyed. He was beginning to like having Art as a friend. They treated each other like buddies, something Denny had never had. He had spent his whole life in the house with his brothers so everyone was treated equally. He knew that he deserved to be treated like a grown-up, and that's just what Art did. To Art, they were just two friends, and it was obvious that Denny felt the same.

"Who wants to go down to the basketball courts?" Art suggested it before realizing that basketball was not an option for the wheelchair-bound kids. "I do," Denny answered. I'll kick your butt in a game, let's go!" On the way there Art tried to think of something for them to do that would be fun for them both. But when they got to the courts, Denny already had ideas.   "We'll play half-court... you play like you always do and I'll roll the ball between a goal. Put those cups down and make a goal for me."

Art began to feel like he'd make a bad choice in bringing this kid to the court. After all, he could get hurt. "Put the ball on the ground and I'll push it with my foot pedals." He began rolling up to the ball and, like a soccer player, pushed the ball toward the goal. "Hey! That's working!" Art was impressed. Running alongside of the wheelchair, Art acted like he was trying to get the ball until Denny hit it one last time, sending it between the two cups on the ground. "He shoots... HE SCORES! See Art, I'm gonna kick your butt!"

Art laughed, impressed with the competitive spirit. Picking up the ball he announced, "If you think I'm going to be easy on you 'cause you're in that chair, you're WRONG buddy!" So there they were, two friends playing basketball, laughing and sassing each other with every step. As Denny rolled the ball along he blurted, "We're buddies, aren't we Art?!"

Art answered proudly, "We sure are, buddy. We sure are."

TRAGEDY STRIKES

After supper Art had some free time and went for a run. The trails through the woods were beautiful, often opening with views of the lake, then just as quickly turning back into dense forest. He thought about the incredible experience he was having. It was amazing to see these incredibly brave kids endure all that they do, without a hint of self-pity. They really were strong, stronger than Art felt he could ever be.

As he ran, his mind drifted to D. He couldn't ignore that she was the prettiest girl he'd ever seen. There were no girls at his school like her. He'd never felt this way before, a yearning feeling took over when he thought of her. She was somehow different. She was so sweet. She was so cool. She was everything.

Getting back to the outskirts of camp, Art could hear a commotion at the nurse's station. Slowing to a jog as he approached the ruckus began to make sense. There was an emergency and someone was in trouble.

Outside of the cabin D was sitting with Michael and Dougie. Seeing Art, D jumped up and ran to him so she wouldn't have to shout. "There's something wrong with Denny! He looked white as a ghost and his breathing went all crazy." Art ran past her and into the cabin.

Nurse Dawn turned around and motioned for him to come beside her. Denny lay out on the bed, his bare chest looking like a birdcage, the bones protruded so that each one was visible. He didn't appear to be awake. "Take this," Nurse Dawn ordered as she shoved something into his hands. "It's an AMBU bag." It was a resuscitation bag that had a hose and face mask connected to it. She took the mask and put it to Denny's face. "I need you to do this…" Art watched as she slowly squeezed the bag in and out, simulating the breathing motion of the lungs. Art could see Denny's chest rise and fall, and realized that he was breathing for him.

Denise ran in and announced to Nurse Dawn "They're here, they're landing right outside!" Art could hear a helicopter setting down gently a mere fifty yards outside of the cabin. Looking back to Denny, Art was relieved to see that his eyes were open. His big brown eyes seemed locked on Art. For another moment Art counted and squeezed the bag until someone behind him said "I'll take over!" The paramedic jumped in front of Art as Art patted Denny quickly, saying, "Be strong, buddy. You're going to be all right…"

Art got swept to the side as the group of paramedics and camp staff rushed by with Denny on a gurney. Art shouted, "I want to go...", but no one seemed to notice. Tears rolled down Art's cheeks as they boarded the chopper and began to take off. The whole scene was surreal. He hadn't noticed that Denise and the other boys had come up and were gathered around him. "He's going to be okay, Art. Let's just pray that he will be okay." The words were soothing to him as he turned and saw D. "He's going to be okay..." Art threw his arms around her and hugged her until he was strong enough to stand on his own again. The boys watched Art with a look of concern. Michael watched the chopper go up into the sky as little Dougie looked away. He was more sensitive than the other boys and tried not to believe what was happening.

When the chopper was out of sight, everyone just sort of stayed still, not knowing what to do next. Joan's voice bellowed out, "Everyone listen up! He's in good hands now and there's nothing we can do but pray. Let's bow our heads for a moment of prayer knowing that he's under God's care, let's just pray that everything will be okay." Most everyone bowed their head. Art noticed how many of the "rollers" did it. They were so young but, for most of them, prayer was already a daily ritual. Art closed his eyes as he felt D's hand slip into his. The moment was magical and real. He prayed for his little buddy and pleaded for his safe return. All the while, D's touch reassured him.

They walked, hand in hand, while Art tried to make sense of it all. "Maybe if we hadn't of played basketball, I shouldn't have let him get so excited." Suddenly D stopped him in his tracks, "You saw how much fun he was having. Dennis was having the time of his life! Besides, his records say he goes to the hospital every other month. Was it your fault all of the other times?"

Art thought for a moment, "His records really say that?"
D squeezed his hand, "Yes, they really say that!" Her stare told him she was telling the truth. She tugged his hand, "Now let's go back, his brothers are probably setting fire to the cabin or something..."

Back at the cabin little Dougie finally spoke. "Is Denny going to be with Jesus?" Art was taken off guard, "No, buddy. No. He's just a little sick and they're going to make him better. Don't worry, just keep hope, okay?" Art went to bed that night thinking the worst, teary eyed and exhausted, he finally slipped into a very sound sleep.

A MOTHER'S TOUGH LOVE

Two whole days went by and there was no word of Denny, only that he was still in the hospital and not able to see visitors. His mother, of course, was by his side. No one at the hospital was big enough to keep her away, not even overnight. She slept by his side, and during the day sat talking to him and telling him to get better.

Mrs. Ferguson's life had been spent raising these children in a small house that she called "the zoo". The kids had always been taught that they were just like everybody else. They were held to standards that made them tough, a trait that she knew they needed to make the most of their struggle.

She fought for their rights with Herculean strength. Denny was still enrolled in the local high school because she wouldn't allow the school to convince her that it would be too "difficult" for him. Denny was going to have all of the challenges and benefits of the outside world as long as he was physically able. She knew the time would come when he would be stuck at home, bedridden in a hospital bed, leaving only for his weekly doctor's appointments or the occasional emergency room visit.

She had become an expert in the medical field, doing research so that she could challenge the doctors, seeing to it that her children were getting the best care possible. Her skills were diverse, and her passion was intense. Anything her children needed to live a "normal" life was provided for them because of her fierce, often stubborn, determination. The lady was a force to be reckoned with.

JOAN'S SURPRISE

Director Joan left the camp one day but no one knew where she was going. She was gone all day until, finally, she returned while everyone was at supper. She walked into the cafeteria and went straight to the front. "Everyone... EVERYONE! I have an announcement to make..."

All of the aides and campers quieted down and looked to the front.

"I've got a surprise for you, and I think you're going to like it!"

Out of the corner of his eye, Art noticed the screen door swing open and a kid in a wheelchair roll through. "DENNY!"

The room erupted in shouting and applause. The kids and adults went crazy with joy. Denny rolled through, smiling a slightly ornery smile. "He's okay," Art shouted at D. "I know! Joan told me this morning. We wanted to surprise you. The doctor's said he could come by to see everybody, but he's going to have to go home tonight." The room was so loud that she found herself shouting at the top of her lungs.

Art and D raced up to see Denny and, after making their way through the crowd, gave him hugs. Michael and Dougie were more interested in the helicopter ride than Denny's well-being. But Denny didn't mind, he told them how cool it was and that he knew he was going to be alright the whole time.

Art remembered seeing some fear in Denny's eyes as they rolled him to the chopper, but didn't question his bravery. One thing he had learned about Denny Ferguson was that he was a tough kid, an amazing kid whose reputation was that of a fearless big brother. And for Michael and Dougie's sake, Art would never suggest otherwise.

THE PARTY'S OVER

On the last day of camp, Art watched all the campers gather for the lowering of the flag. Michael didn't take part but didn't seem to mind. Art's eyes were full of tears, though he did his best to hide it. Director Joan stepped beside him and knew just what he was thinking. "These kids look forward to this week all year long, one week to go wild and forget about their battles. I can't help but look out and wonder how many will make it back next year.

Sometimes they surprise you. They're resilient and make it through another year when all odds are against them. Other times a kid that seemed just fine one year doesn't show up again. But the beautiful thing is that all of these kids have each other. They make friends that they cherish all year long and look forward to seeing the next time around. You kids did great, Art. You and Denise and all of the volunteers that made this year special. Thank you."

Art looked at Joan and gave her a hug, "No, Joan, thank you."

All of the campers were buzzing around getting last minute addresses, vowing to stay in touch with their newfound friends. Art saw D through the crowd and waited for her eyes to meet his. Tilting his head, he summoned her away from the bustling crowd. "You want to go down to the dock one last time?"
"Yeah, that'd be nice..."

Neither spoke as they walked along the wooded path. D noticed that Art was crying and hiding it by looking away. Reaching out, she held his hand in hers and bumped him playfully. Neither said a word until they reached the old wooden pier. Art stared out at the lake, "How can you be so strong at a time like this?" D took his face in her hands and turned it toward her. Only then did Art see her tears.

"And to think, I almost didn't come to this camp! I wouldn't have met the boys... I wouldn't have met you..."
D tilted her head, resting it on Art's shoulder. "I know. The kids were great. You just gotta love 'em. And they really look up to you, Art."
Art shrugged, "They weren't sure about you at first,

but they sure love you now! You were wonderful with them."

"*We* were wonderful with them…" They stood gazing out at the lake, its mirror smooth surface so beautiful that Art wished they could stand there forever.
Taken by the moment, Art turned to D. "Before we go back I've just got to tell you… I want to tell you…" D squeezed his hands and pulled him closer, "What? You want to tell me what, Art?" He looked into her beautiful brown eyes and realized that words weren't enough. Without another thought, he kissed her.
For a moment they stood, holding hands and kissing. D seemed so comfortable that Art didn't even feel awkward. It was just right. There, on the dock of Bear Lake Camp, Art fell in love.

Suddenly giggling, D pulled Art by the hand, "We'd better get back and say goodbye to the kids." Art was silent. Sadness took his breath away as he realized that it was all coming to an end.

THEN LIFE HAPPENED

When camp was over Art was able to keep in touch with the boys. The Ferguson family moved to Fort Wayne to be closer to its highly acclaimed hospital.

After high school graduation the old gang went their separate ways. Art quickly moved away from Fort Wayne, feeling that he had been raised to "leave the nest". Over the years he'd visit the boys and send gifts from distant locations until, one by one, as Dougie would say, each "went to be with Jesus".

Joan had said on the first day of camp, "You're heart will be paid ten-fold by the end of the week", these words had become a reality for young Art and stayed with him always.

He never returned to Bear Lake Camp, and never saw Denise again. It made his heart ache to think of her but the memories stayed with him and his love for her never diminished. She would always be the love that slipped away, and the Ferguson boys, Denny, Michael and Dougie, would forever be the angels that watched over them.

The years passed, friends fell out of touch, and the old neighborhood became a fond memory for Art and the others that were fortunate enough to live there. Art always thought his experiences there would make for a great book, but that's a dream he kept to himself.

THE PAST REVISITED

The oldie's hour ended just as Arthur turned the corner onto Milton Street. The deejay's voice boomed through the speakers until Arthur turned the volume down. He didn't want the distraction. It had been years since he'd seen these familiar surroundings, and both he and the neighborhood had changed. The trees had grown tall and the alleys had been paved over. Many of the houses had been repainted or torn down, and a new shopping center took the place of Hankey's Lot. The gentle rain patted the windshield as he pulled into the driveway of the old Lohsie House. It looked eerie nestled in the overgrown woods. The broken windows were a sign that kids still wandered onto the property, uninvited. Graffiti covered the front door, which was half open and falling off of its hinges.

Art walked around the house, solemnly scanning the area that had once brought him so much dread. He remembered how terrified he was each time he raced through the woods, thinking that the old man would surely kill him if he were to get caught there.

In the distance was a patch of overgrowth that nature had taken back. Art recognized it right away.

"The old woodpile..." Art muttered. Looking at it, he remembered the terror that they had felt the day Phil got his foot stuck there. The memories of the old gang and good times swirled in his head. He looked in the direction of the fence, half expecting to hear the bully's voice urging him on. As he approached the back steps of the house his eyes fell upon a familiar sight. Climbing the steps, cautiously, reverently, he stared back into his childhood. A lone baseball sat ominously on the top step, weather beaten and motionless.

Searching his coat pocket for his cell phone, Art chuckled as he pressed the keys. "Phil, this is Arthur Carlson. I know it's been awhile but you are never going to believe where I am. I'm at Lohsie's Woods! We've got to get together while I'm in town, buddy." Art's heart jumped for joy as he reached down and picked up the baseball. "And Phil, I've got something for you, something special."

As Arthur Carlson walked up the driveway toward his car he realized that he had finally grown up. Because, this time, he didn't have to run away from Lohsie's Woods.

EPILOGUE - THE LEGEND IS PASSED DOWN

Years have passed since Old Man Lohsie lived in the woods of Fort Wayne, Indiana. But even today, children sometimes notice an old man standing at the broken window of the old abandoned house, watching each child in search of the bully among them. Some nights they hear the sound of an old clunker rambling into the driveway and fading out as if driving into the old garage one last time. But the garage is no more. Mr. Lohsie no longer lives in the decrepit house in the woods, except in the minds of a new generation of neighborhood children.

The children that knew Lohsie firsthand have grown up and started their own families. And each night, as they tuck their kids into bed, they tell them scary bedtime stories about the old man in the woods... they tell them the legend of Lohsie's Woods.

THE END

JUST FOR FUN...

Sample Question: What was Arthur's nickname?

Answer: Art

PART ONE – LOHSIE'S WOODS

1) How old was the song on the radio?

2) In what city was Arthur born?

3) The kids were warned to stay out of what place?

4) What is the bully's name?

5) Which one was "a born vandal"?

6) Where did Art hide when he ran from Old Man Lohsie?

7) Who had all of the coolest toys?

8) What was Bauer's dad building for him?

9) What kind of tree was in Bauer's Yard?

10) Who got left holding the bat when Bauer vandalized Mr. Hankey's fence?

11) To save his own tail, who "snitched" on Bauer?

12) Who got his foot caught in the woodpile?

13) What got left at the woodpile that Bauer wanted back?

14) What was Art's "mission"?

15) What did Art learn about Mr. Lohsie?

PART TWO - THE NEW KID

1) When the kids played hide-and-seek, what was considered "out of bounds"?

2) What were the kids playing when the moving van arrived?

3) The kids looked up to the neighborhood sports hero. What was his name?

4) What was the new kid's name?

5) What was his sister's name?

6) What was in the new kid's backyard?

7) What was the name of Arthur's school?

8) What was the name of Phil's school?

9) What was special about Johnny?

10) What was Abe Alton?

11) Who was Mary Alton?

12) What did Johnny's mom give the boys as a reward for being nice to Johnny?

13) How did the boys feel about that?

14) What did they do with the money?

15) What would you have done in that situation?

PART THREE – MAGIC AT BIG TONY'S

1) What is the name of the new pizza shop?

2) What was Big Tony's Snack?

3) What is so amazing about Big Tony?

4) What did Art's mom put in the attic?

5) What will happen to Phil if he gets into trouble?

6) Why did the kids tease Art when he went back to school?

7) What scary dish did Arthur's mom make him for supper?

8) What scary place did the boys walk by on the way to the pizza shop?

9) What prank did the boys play on Big Tony?

10) What holiday is on October 31st? (Hint: Boo!)

11) What name didn't Art like to be called?

12) Why was Art's mom surprised to see him sitting at the kitchen table?

13) Who helped Art with Math problems?

14) Who did Art's parents invite to their Halloween party?

15) Was Big Tony really a giant?

PART FOUR - BEAR LAKE CAMP

1) What was special about the campers at Bear Lake Camp?

2) Why did Art volunteer?

3) What was the camp director's name?

4) What was the word used to describe campers that were in wheelchairs?

5) What was the word used to describe campers that were not in wheelchairs?

6) What was the name of the camp nurse?

7) What were the names of the Ferguson boys?

8) Who was "the brown-eyed girl"?

9) Which Ferguson boy had the honor of raising the flag?

10) What was wrong with the camp director's cabin door?

11) What kind of car did the camp director dream of getting?

12) Art and which camper played basketball?

13) When the camper got sick, what came to take him to the hospital?

14) What was so special about Mrs. Ferguson?

15) What should you say if you meet someone in a wheelchair?

PART ONE - LOHSIE'S WOODS

1) 30 years
2) Fort Wayne, Indiana
3) Lohsie's Woods
4) Mitch Bauer
5) Bauer
6) In a tree
7) Bauer
8) A tree house
9) An apple tree
10) Art!
11) Art
12) Phil
13) His baseball bat
14) to get baseballs off of Mr. Lohsie's porch
15) that he was not a monster as Bauer had said. Bauer the bully had been lying about the old man to scare the other kids.

PART TWO - THE NEW KIDS

1) The woods around Mr. Lohsie's house
2) Football
3) Brad Bergman
4) Johnny Alton
5) Maggie
6) A trampoline
7) Abbott School
8) Zion School
9) He had special needs and was in Special Education classes
10) Johnny's dad
11) Johnny's mom
12) Money
13) Excited at first, then guilty
14) They bought a football for Johnny
15) Only you know the answer to that question!

PART THREE - MAGIC AT BIG TONY'S

1) Big Tony's Pizza

2) The largest size of pizza (Giant size!)

3) He is a Giant

4) A mysterious box

5) He'll get grounded

6) He believed he saw a Giant

7) Ghoul-ash!

8) Lohsie's Woods

9) wrote on his windows with shaving cream

10) Halloween!

11) Arthur

12) He was doing his homework

13) Becky the cheerleader

14) The Bauer's

15) No

PART FOUR - BEAR LAKE CAMP

1) Most of them were in wheelchairs

2) To meet girls

3) Joan

4) Rollers

5) Walkers

6) Dawn

7) Denny, Michael, and Dougie

8) Denise (Nickname: D)

9) Michael

10) It was rusty and slammed shut

11) Volkswagen Beetle (Nickname: Bug)

12) Denny

13) a helicopter

14) She raised three kids with Muscular Dystrophy and fought for their rights and needs

15) The same thing you'd say to anyone else... Hello!

Made in the USA
Charleston, SC
10 November 2010